RAY GREY

Born with no weather magic.

NEVER gives up!

Wants to be an Earth Explorer just like La Blaze DeLight.

SNOWDEN EVERFREEZE

The cleverest Snow Weatherling in Sky Academy!

Never goes anywhere without his *Anthology of Snowflakes*.

Loves a drizzle-pickle sandwich.

DROPLETT DEWBELLS

Uses her rain weather magic to puddle-port.

NEVER does her homework.

Will SPLOSH anyone who's mean to her friends!

NIM

Was adopted by Ray since he couldn't be a proper cloud.

Often explodes without warning.

Loves Ray with all his floofy heart.

LA BLAZE DELIGHT

An Earth explorer and adventurer.

Never seen without her trusty pigeon sidekick, Coo La La.

Possesses the rarest sun weather magic.

HAZE AND CLOUDIA GREY

Ray's mum and dad!

Haze always brings human treasures home for Ray.

Cloudia is constantly mending Cloud Nine's silver lining.

CLOUDIMULUS SUBURBS

SUNKEEPER CONSERVATORY

FLURRY MOUNTAINS

SUNFLOWER FIELD

BROLLY LANES

DRIPPING-DOWN VILLAGE

CRACKLING CAVES

VALLEY OF WINDS

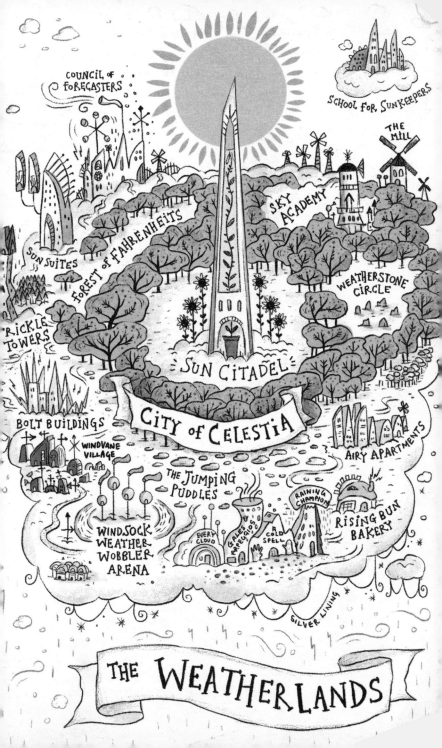

CHAPTER 1
NOT ONE SMIDGE

Every cloud really DOES have a silver lining. And if you lived on Cloud Nine like Ray Grey, the silver lining was always getting tangled or ending up in a twist. Mostly because Ray and her cloud-cat Nim kept getting caught in it.

Ray sighed as she dangled from the silvery threads like a puppet. 'I'm going to be late for Sky Academy AGAIN!'

Once Nim had chewed his way through the silver thread, the ten-year-old Weatherling with odd-coloured eyes (one purple and one blue) finally broke free.

'Just a bit faster, Nim!' said Ray as they soared across the Weatherlands, zipping past the snow-covered Flurry Mountains. 'Then we can grab our morning cake from the Rising Bun Bakery!'

Nim miaowed and farted a tiny cloud in response. He often exploded, and Ray was hoping against hope that this fart didn't lead to a bigger explosion and make her even later.

Ray gripped Nim's back a little tighter as they approached the Valley of Winds, where they were buffeted about rather ungracefully. This part of the journey was VERY bumpy, and Ray was quite sure her knickers were on show, but she didn't mind too much as she was wearing her favourite pair covered with sparkly stars.

Finally, the wind died down and the hills opened up to reveal the City of Celestia.

Odd-shaped houses, a mishmash of quirky shops and higgledy-piggledy streets wound their way around the Forest of Fahrenheits. In the centre of the forest stood the pointiest and shiniest building – the Sun Citadel, where the mighty SunKeepers powered the BIG glowing Sunflower in the sky and gave the Earth its light.

Ray breathed in the scent of freshly baked treats and sweet snowdrop syrup coming from the Rising

Bun Bakery below and wondered if she had JUST enough time to grab a tasty treat. The Sky Academy wind chime hadn't jingled yet after all, and she could *never* resist a lightning scone with a big dollop of skyberry jam on top.

Ray guided Nim downwards. Just when she thought that their landing was going to be smooth for once, Nim exploded a few metres from the ground, sending Ray roly-polying straight through the bakery entrance.

'AH, RAY! MY FAVOURITE LITTLE CUSTOMER!' said a very large, jolly-looking man in an apron. 'ONE O' THESE DAYS YOU'LL LAND ON YER FEET!'

'Good morning, Slap!' Ray said with a grin, rubbing her bottom. Baker Slap was a Thunder Weatherling with fists the size of tree trunks: perfect for creating mighty booms of thunder AND kneading dough.

Ray clambered to her feet and skipped over to the counter. It was full to the brim with beautifully decorated cakes and pretty pastries that crackled and oozed and bubbled. She stroked Nim as the cloud-cat drifted over to join her. He'd recovered from his explosion, but now his eyes were stuck to his bottom.

'ANY SIGN OF THAT MAGIC YET, LITTLE ONE?' asked Baker Slap with a wink. He asked Ray the same question every day, and every time, the answer was:

'Nope! Not one smidge!'

Ray Grey wasn't like all the other Weatherlings. While they all had a form of powerful weather magic – sun, snow, rain, wind, cloud and thunder 'n' lightning – Ray didn't have any. In fact, there hadn't been weather magic on her mother's side of the family for *generations*. Ray thought that maybe, just maybe, she'd wake up one morning and miraculously a little HINT of weather magic MIGHT appear. But there hadn't been one drop of rain, or floof of cloud, or flurry of snow. Nim seemed to possess more wafts of wind than Ray did magic, and he was just a cloud-cat with a tendency to explode.

'WELL, Y'KNOW WHAT I FINK, RAY,' said Slap. 'I FINK YOU GOT THE BEST MAGIC OF 'EM ALL . . .'

'Really?' said Ray, feeling slightly confused.

'YOU GOT A BIG 'EART!' said Slap, putting a hand to his chest.

Ray giggled. 'Well, my heart might be big, but my tummy is bigger and wishes it could eat all the cakes here!'

'WHICH ONE DO YOU FANCY TODAY?' asked Baker Slap, leaning his HUGE body across the counter.

'Hmmm,' Ray pondered. 'I *thought* I was going to order a lightning scone, but that was until I spotted THOSE.' She pointed to a row of bright blue buns she'd never seen before.

'OH! THESE ARE BRAND-NEW BAKES WE MADE 'SPECIALLY FOR THE ECLIPSE FESTIVAL TONIGHT!' said Slap.

'Even better!' said Ray happily.

A lady's face covered in flour popped out from the back kitchen and waved. 'Hey, Ray!'

'Hi, Streak!' Ray replied.

Streak was Slap's sister – the lightning sibling of the pair, as pointy as Slap was round. She had a knack of zapping scones to absolute perfection. 'I see you spotted the rumblebuns!' she said with an excitable grin. 'Wanna be the FIRST Weatherling to try one?!'

Nim, who had somehow grown an extra cloud head, miaowed happily.

'I think that's a YES from both of us!' said Ray, licking her lips.

Baker Slap scooped up two of the bright blue buns before popping them on to a napkin. 'THERE YOU ARE LITTLE ONE,' he boomed. 'NO CHARGE!'

'Thank you so much!' said Ray, putting away

the sky coins her mum had given her that morning.

Nim was quick to lap up his rumblebun in one almighty GULP, but Ray gasped as her blue cake began to wobble around in her palm. Baker Slap gave a hearty chuckle as a deep rumble came from the dough and a small bead of bright pink syrup oozed from the top.

'YA DIDN'T FINK IT WAS CALLED A RUMBLEBUN FOR NUFFIN', DID YA?!' he said. 'BEST EAT IT UP BEFORE IT ERUPTS!'

Ray bit into her rumblebun quickly, savouring the syrupy skyberry sweetness and the sour snowdrop.

'*Thish ish delishush!*' she said through a mouthful.

DING-ALING-ALING-ALING-ALIIIIIING!

'That's the first school warning chime. I'd better dash!' said Ray, quickly gobbling down the rest of her rumblebun.

Nim expanded until he was roughly the size of a large bed and Ray hopped up on to his back.

'SEE YA AT THE ECLIPSE FESTIVAL TONIGHT?' asked Baker Slap as he waved goodbye.

'You bet!' called Ray. 'I can't wait! It'll be our first Eclipse!'

But little did Ray know that her first Eclipse would change her life FOREVER . . .

CHAPTER 2

SNOWDEN EVERFREEZE

Ray guided Nim across the Forest of Fahrenheits, ready to meet her best friends Snowden and Droplett at the Weatherstone Circle before school. Although it was usually just Snowden, since Droplett was never on time.

'Ready to land without exploding this time, Nim?' said Ray.

Nim nodded and miaowed happily. Then he exploded.

Once again, Ray found herself tumbling to the ground . . . landing bottom first in a patch of sparkly silver flowers called Snowpogglian Dalooloos, which erupted with a flurry of little white-winged bugs.

Ray groaned and scrambled to her feet, wondering how many bruises her poor bottom now had. She loved Nim, but she really wished he would explode a teeny bit less.

'Well, at least I landed in the right place.' Ray was in the centre of the Weatherstone Circle. She had always felt a strong connection to it, despite her lack of weather magic. The six Weatherstones had been there for as long as anyone could remember, covered in bright pink moss and tiny white flowers. Each had a unique symbol carved into its front, representing a type of weather magic and the instrument used to channel it.

Ray often wondered what kind of weather magic she *could* have had. She loved the thought of using a flowing cape to create beautiful rain magic, just like her friend Droplett. A thunder drum or a lightning stick sounded fun, although, given Ray's clumsiness, she wasn't sure if something as loud or electrical would be a great choice – not to mention the fact she needed a thunder or lightning twin to complete the set.

DING-ALING-ALING-ALING-ALIIIIIING!

The second Sky Academy wind chime jingled through the woods, snapping Ray out of her wistful weather dream.

'Yikes, I'd better hurry up and find Nim!' she said. Brushing herself down, she pulled a bewildered Snowpogglian bug out of her nostril. 'NIIIIIIIM!' she called. 'Where are you?!'

She spotted a patch of puff pods.

'Hmmm, I wonder if he's in there . . .'

She was careful not to disturb

the puff pods as she searched through. Inside each pod was a baby cloud-creature ready to be picked by a CloudWeatherling on their first birthday and become their lifelong cloud-companion.

Nim was MEANT to be someone's cloud-companion, but he was born with a rare glitch, making him change shape or explode without warning. When Ray found the tiny cloud-kitten wandering all alone in the forest, she decided to adopt him. Since neither of them could contribute to the world of weather magic, they made the perfect pair!

After no luck in the patch of puff pods, Ray ended up crawling through a bed of tall and VERY STICKY stalks. One of the long stalks snapped, spurting a thick purple gloop all over Ray's face.

'BLEURGH!' cried Ray, desperately trying to wipe the gooey substance from her cheeks.

'Ray? Is that you?' said

a voice, making her jump.

A kind-faced boy with curly white hair and shiny purple glasses was standing behind Ray, cradling Nim's head in his arms.

'I found a bit of your cat,' he said with a wonky smile.

'Snowden!' cried Ray. 'Nim exploded – again! – and now I'm covered in this yucky goo from that plant. It won't come off!'

Snowden tapped his chin. A trail of snowflakes – or, as Snowden liked to call them, THINK-flakes – erupted from his left ear. This always happened when he was pondering.

'Ah yes, that's a Stenchamite Stalk,' he said. 'They contain the stickiest sap!'

'I've just worked that out the hard way,' said Ray. Her hands were now firmly stuck together.

As Ray finally pulled her hands apart, Snowden reached for one of the stalks and wrenched it out of the ground, root and all. He kept the whole thing intact before slipping it into his satchel. 'Never know when the sticky sap might come in handy!' he said with a wink.

Nim's floofy bottom suddenly appeared with a POOF in Ray's arms.

'Welcome back, Nim!' chuckled Snowden, helping Ray to reassemble the cloud-cat.

'That'll do!' said Ray, even though Nim was now just a head and bottom. Nim seemed happy enough. The rest of him would drift back at some stage.

'So, I had to make up a brand-new snow spell for my homework,' said Snowden as the friends strode through the forest towards Sky Academy. 'Can I test it out on you quickly, just to be extra sure it works?'

Ray raised her eyebrows, then said with a glint in

her eye: 'SNOW problem with me!'

'Oh, Ray . . .' said Snowden, shaking
his head.

He adjusted his snow gloves, which
were covered with beautiful and intricately
embroidered patterns. Each unique pair of snow
gloves enabled their owner to channel their
snow magic properly.

Ray watched as Snowden drew a snowflake
in the air with his finger. First, he created the
arms of the beautiful snowflake, before adding
dashes and dots and flicks. He stepped back,
looking satisfied as his finished
pattern hung in mid-air.
The snowflake then
morphed into a ribbon
of icy sparkles that
danced around

Ray's head before turning into a tall and very extravagant snow wig.

Ray burst out laughing and did a little twirl. 'I might not be able to MAKE any weather magic,' she said, 'but I can definitely WEAR IT WITH STYLE!'

Snowden grinned and bowed.

The snow wig slowly started to melt and drip down Ray's neck, making her shiver.

'Sorry,' Snowden added. 'It still needs work.' He flourished his gloved hand to make the wig disappear into a shower of sparkles.

'Well, Snowden Everfreeze, I think it's *amazing*,' said Ray, linking arms with her best friend. 'You're so clever!'

Snowden shrugged modestly. 'I have Granny

Everfreeze to thank for insisting I learn at least one snow spell every night before bed,' he said, tapping the HUGE book wedged into his satchel. Snowden never went anywhere without his trusty *Anthology of Snowflakes*. 'Gran says if I want to be a successful Forecaster when I grow up, I have to know every snowflake off by heart.'

Ray let out a long whistle. 'There must be THOUSANDS in there,' she said, poking the humungous book. 'But if anyone's good enough to be a GREAT Forecaster making lovely snowy weather on Earth, it's you!'

Ray knew that she could never be a Forecaster or anything that required magic. But it didn't matter. Because when she grew up, she wanted to be JUST like her favourite Earth Explorer, La Blaze DeLight! La Blaze explored planet Earth, discovering human treasures and writing books about them. Ray had read ALL of La Blaze's books. And thanks to her dad's job, she had already started to collect her OWN weird and wonderful human treasures. Her current favourite was a paperclip she had framed on her bedroom wall.

The final school wind chime rang through the Forest of Fahrenheits with a DING-ALING-ALING-ALING-ALIIIIIING!

'Better hurry!' said Snowden.

The friends rushed through a trail of bright red windshrooms that blew out sparkly orange smoke, hopped over a row of prickly puddles and dodged a nibbling nimbleweed.

'Looks like Droplett is going to be late *again*,' said Snowden, looking around for their friend as they approached the Sky Academy entrance.

SPLOSH!

Ray and Snowden found themselves SOAKED with water as a puddle appeared in front of them from which a small, spiky-haired girl emerged. She grinned and said, 'I think you'll find that Droplett Dewbells – FUTURE PUDDLE-PORTING PROFESSIONAL – is RIGHT on time!'

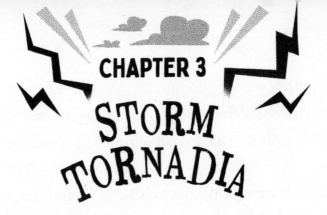

CHAPTER 3
STORM TORNADIA

'One of these days I'll start school without being drenched,' sighed Snowden, wiping his face with his scarf. Droplett put her hands on her hips.

'Don't count on it!' she said. She gave the two friends a big hug and swished her rain cape again, causing another stream of water to knock Snowden's glasses off.

Droplett was Ray's other best friend. She was very different to Snowden, bursting with energy and exceedingly good at puddle-porting or any type of rain-related sports. As well as being a mischievous fidget-bottom, Droplett was an extremely loyal friend.

Ray, Snowden and Droplett joined the crowd of Weatherlings bustling into the higgledy-piggledy school building. Sky Academy had been around for so long that it had almost become part of the forest: a mishmash of roofs, observatories, masts and balconies, all intertwined within the ancient tree trunks. Here, young Weatherlings learned all they needed to know about weather magic and how to use it. Except for the Sun Weatherlings, who trained at a special school for SunKeepers.

Above the highest dome was the Sky Academy emblem, shining proudly in the sunlight.

Young Weatherlings of all ages were hurrying to their classes, surfing on their wind instruments or running along snowy stepping stones. Some were using lightning webs to scale the walls and leap straight through the windows.

'Are you both going to the Eclipse Festival tonight?' asked Droplett as the friends and Nim made their way up to their morning classroom.

'A windillion times YES!' cried Ray. 'I can't wait! It only happens ONCE every eleven years, so I wouldn't miss it for the skies! Are you?'

'Of course!' said Snowden. 'Just as soon as I finish my homework.'

'I won't be doing ANY homework,' said Droplett.

'You never do,' Snowden added, half smiling.

The friends took their seats at the back of the first-year classroom. Nim sat himself next to Ray. Complicated-looking dials and gauges decorated the walls, while barometers and thermometers were perched along the side benches.

Ray's teacher Mr Windbreaker blew into his wind trumpet, sending a light breeze around the room to get the students' attention. He was incredibly old, with frizzy tufts of hair protruding from his ears.

'I'm sure you're all very excited about the Eclipse Festival tonight,' said Mr Windbreaker. 'But we must try to concentrate. Your Harvest Moon exams are coming up very soon, and there's still lots to learn!'

Everyone groaned, apart from Snowden, who loved exams.

Morning classes at Sky Academy often involved studying subjects such as Weather History, Earth Studies (Ray's favourite), Temperature Training (BORING) and General Weather Knowledge.

Then the first years split up to practise their own weather magic – apart from Ray, who went to the library to read instead.

'Let's get started!' said the teacher, clapping his hands. 'Please take out your Weather History textbooks, and have your notepads ready.'

'Ugh, Weather History!' moaned Droplett. 'Why do we need to learn about stuff that already happened?'

Snowden's left ear erupted with a satisfying POP of think-flakes. 'It's VERY important,' he said softly. 'It's good to know how our world developed and changed, and learn from the past.'

Droplett stared at Snowden, then shook her head. 'Sorry, I think I might have dozed off with my eyes open,' she said sarcastically, before grinning.

'Enough chitter chatter! Let's get started!' trilled the teacher, stepping on his floating wind trumpet. 'As we know, the Earth's weather is carefully planned and carried out by the Council of Forecasters to ensure a PERFECT balance.

HOWEVER . . .' He paused for dramatic effect. 'We all know that for every snowfall, every drizzle, every waft of wind, there is another kind of Weatherling lurking around the corner, ready to cause trouble and MESS UP those weather plans . . .'

A pointy-faced girl with green hair swept across her face put her hand up straight away.

'Yes, Frazzle?' asked Mr Windbreaker.

'*ROGUES, sir, they don't make weather like the norm,*' said Frazzle Striker.

'*They prefer to make a big bad STORM,*' said her thunder brother Fump, who was sitting next to her.

'A perfect answer, Frazzle . . . and Fump. Well done!' said Mr Windbreaker.

Frazzle smirked and Fump puffed his chest out.

'Dripping drainpipes,' sighed Droplett, rolling her eyes.

Frazzle and Fump Striker were thunder 'n' lightning twins, although Fump looked like a stretched and rather squashed version of his sister. They loved to be the centre of attention, and ALWAYS spoke in rhyme. The twins were also the meanest kids in school.

The teacher slowly floated around the room on his wind trumpet.

'Rogues, Rogues, Rogues,' he trilled. 'They refuse to use instruments to channel their weather magic, making it chaotic, unpredictable and destructive. They have created some of the WORST weather the Earth has ever seen. What do we call a group of Rogues working together?'

Ray put her hand up. 'A storm?' she said.

'A stoooorm!' Mr Windbreaker repeated with emphasis. 'The Earth has seen some terrible storms. And every storm is named after the Rogue who planned it, such as Storm Lindsey, Storm Cracklesworth and Storm Bob. Storm Bob was bad. BUT, since we are celebrating a Sunflower Eclipse tonight, I thought it appropriate for today's lesson to focus on one particular Eclipse just over a thousand years ago; one that marked the beginnings of the biggest and baddest storm Earth has ever known . . . STORM TORNADIA!'

'We all know about that storm,' said Snowden with a shudder.

Mr Windbreaker whizzed across the length of the room theatrically on his wind trumpet. 'Tornadia Twist was one of the worst Rogues in history. Her storm went on for a whole century. During that time, the sun didn't shine at all.'

'That's *so* spooky!' said Droplett with an excitable wriggle.

'Storm Tornadia marked the end of an era for Celestia AND Earth,' said the teacher. 'We have very few records of those dark times, but it is said this storm saw the extinction of a whole other group of Weatherlings.'

The students gasped.

'Hold on,' said Droplett, counting on her fingers. 'Sun, snow, rain, cloud, wind, thunder 'n' lightning. What other kind of Weatherling is there?'

'It is believed that a seventh kind of

Weatherling lived among us here in Celestia,' said Mr Windbreaker. 'Weatherlings with a mysterious weather magic unlike anyone else: the ability to make colours known as RAINBOWS stretch across the sky!'

The class muttered among themselves in hushed whispers.

Ray furrowed her eyebrows. 'I thought rainbows were just made up?' she whispered.

'I've never even heard of them!' said Droplett.

'Rainbow weather magic is *ancient* weather history,' whispered Snowden. 'Nobody really knows much about it, or if the Rainbow Weatherlings existed at all.'

'Well, I'm surprised YOU don't know all about it,' said Droplett, flicking a raindrop at Snowden's nose. 'You know EVERYTHING!'

'That's not true,' Snowden replied. 'I only know *almost* everything.'

'SIR!' Frazzle blurted, waving her hand around in the air. '*I HAVE heard of rainbows before!*'

'*But whether they were real, we just weren't*

sure!' finished Fump.

'You may or may NOT believe they existed at all,' said Mr Windbreaker. 'But whatever the case, *rainbow* weather magic – and Rainbow Weatherlings – are no more.'

'But, sir!' called out Droplett. 'What did rainbow weather magic actually do?'

'Well,' said Mr Windbreaker. 'It has been over a thousand years since the Rainbow Weatherlings disappeared. But it IS said that rainbow weather magic was the most POWERFUL and unique of ALL the types of weather magic.'

'Personally, I can't see what's more powerful than a good bit of wind!' Percy McWhoosh shouted out with a chuckle.

Frazzle scoffed. '*Thunder 'n' lightning is most powerful BY FAR.*'

'*With a flick and a thump you always know where WE are!*' said Fump, proudly tapping the thunder drum strapped to his shoulders.

'Whatever the Rainbow Weatherling's magic could do, it is said to have been a GREAT threat to the Rogues,' Mr Windbreaker continued. He glided to the front of the classroom.

'*Pah! They all sound made up to me!*' Frazzle shouted out.

'*Nothing but a silly kids' story!*' said Fump with a wide grin.

The teacher frowned. 'Whether you believe it or not does not change the fact that the weather has never been the same since Storm Tornadia. Whether or not that has anything to DO with the disappearance of this mysterious rainbow weather magic, we will never know.'

Frazzle and Fump rolled their eyes.

'ANYWAY,' barked the teacher, making everyone jump. 'Please open your textbooks to page 132. You'll find a passage on some of the worst Rogues in history. I'd like you to pick a Rogue and write five hundred words about their most famous storm and how the Weather Warriors managed to tame it. You have one hour.'

'Those blasted Rogues need a good hard *splosh* on the bottom!' said Droplett while drawing moustaches over all the pictures in her textbook.

'I think it takes more than a splosh on the bottom to stop a Rogue!' said Ray with a chuckle. 'I wish we knew more about these super powerful Rainbow Weatherlings. Sounds like they gave the Rogues a run for their money.'

'I guess we'll never know,' said Droplett. 'Anyway, I'm more interested in THIS joker!' She poked a photo of an infamous Snow Rogue (who now sported a large scribbled moustache and half-moon glasses). 'Eddie Blizzard,' she read aloud. 'Known for freezing shut ALL the toilet seats of London during the Big Freeze of 1795.' Droplett gave an impressed nod, then glanced at Ray. 'Some might say this Rogue was BOG standard! Eh?! EH?!'

The friends fell about laughing. Nim got overexcited and ended up exploding ALL over the back row, and the rest of the lesson was spent scraping him off the walls.

CHAPTER 4
BIZARRE BUT BEAUTIFUL

While everyone else was off practising their weather magic for the afternoon, Ray took herself to the Lower Sky Library in the basement.

All of the books in the library were stacked upon hundreds of thick tree roots that wove around the walls, and tiny cloud-helpers floated around, ready to fetch any books that you might need from the higher roots.

Ray loved it here and she LOVED books, even though it always took her much longer than her friends to read. The letters on the page got a bit jumbled and jumped about so it was always a challenge. But she never gave up.

Ray always reminded herself of a line she had read in a book by her absolute hero La Blaze DeLight – '*If at first the path you take is bumpy,*

there's always another way! It may take a little
longer, but you'll get there in the end.'

Ray smiled. 'I'll get there in the end,' she said
to herself.

Ray decided to look for a book about the
mysterious Rainbow Weatherlings. But after a long
search, she only found one VERY old and tattered
book called *The Magic of Rainbows*. Ray could just
about make out an illustration of a lady with long,
stripy hair on the cover. She was holding a weather
instrument, but the image was
too faded to see it clearly.

She opened the book
but almost every page
was missing!

On one of the few worn pages that were left was a picture of a multicoloured rainbow stretching across a snowy landscape, with a crowd of humans pointing and smiling and hugging each other.

Ray turned to a double page showing a world map, faded but still visible. Ray loved a good map, especially an Earth map. The shapes of the countries were so interesting, and there were so many mountains, forests, deserts and oceans. But this time one thing in particular caught her eye.

Scribbled on the map was a big, fat cross.

'Look, Nim!' gasped Ray.

The cloud-cat purred and pressed his face up against the page, flattening his nose. Ray took a closer look at the location of the cross. She had to concentrate hard on the letters.

'*The . . . Oldest Tree . . . in the World . . .*' Ray read out. 'How exciting! I wonder if the cross means there's treasure buried there?'

DING-ALING-ALING-ALING-ALIIIIIING! sang the Sky Academy wind chime, marking the end of the school day. Ray hadn't realised she'd spent so long looking at the book. She simply HAD to take it home!

She picked out another two books about her favourite Earth Explorer – *A DeLightful Distance* and *Shiny Things I Found* by La Blaze DeLight – and skipped over to the librarian, Mr Gusty Gavin, who had his nose buried in a book called *Why My Raindrops Turned Green* by Dr Hugh Miditty.

'Hello, Ray!' said Gavin. 'What book has tickled your temperature today?'

Ray slid the books on to the large wooden desk. 'Just these three, please.'

'Haven't you already read these books by La Blaze over fifty times?' asked Gavin with a chuckle.

'Over one hundred times actually!' said Ray with a big smile. 'I just love her so much. I'm going to be an Earth Explorer JUST like La Blaze when I grow up!'

'Well, I'm sure you'll achieve your dream!' said Gavin.

He tickled Nim under the chin, making the cloud-cat roll over happily, leaving his head behind.

Gavin picked up the *The Magic of Rainbows* book next. 'Billowing breezes, this is an ancient one! I don't think it's been borrowed for quite some time. It's falling apart!' he said, wiping the dust off the cover with his sleeve. 'Rainbows, eh? I've heard of those. A bizarre form of weather magic, aren't they?'

Ray nodded. 'Bizarre, but beautiful,' she said.

Gavin looked around and pushed the pile of books towards Ray. 'I tell you what,' he whispered. 'Why don't you just keep them? You're the only one who ever reads La Blaze's adventures, and nobody will miss the rainbow book – it's definitely seen better days!'

'Really?!' asked Ray.

He winked. 'Of course!'

'Thank you so much!' said Ray. 'It must be my lucky day. I got a free rumblebun from the Rising Bun Bakery this morning too!'

'That IS lucky!' said the librarian. 'And I bet you're excited to see your first Eclipse tonight to top it all off?!'

'Oh yes!' said Ray. 'It'll be the first time I've seen the Weatherlands get dark! I'm trying to imagine what it'll be like when the big Sunflower gets covered by the Moon Cheese!' She closed her eyes. 'Probably a bit like THIS!'

'You're in for a treat, young Ray,' said Gavin. 'I've seen a couple of these Eclipses. The last one was just before you were born!'

'What's it like?' asked Ray.

'WELL,' began Gavin. 'These beauuuutiful twinkly specks called STARS fill the whole sky. Then you'll see the great Moon King with his large plate of big round cheese. He dances around, using the big cheese wheel to cover up the old Sunflower while the SunKeepers prepare a new one to glow for the next eleven years.'

Ray wriggled in excitement. Today was turning out to be the best day EVER!

When Ray arrived home on Cloud Nine in the cosy Cloudimulus suburbs, her mother Cloudia Grey was outside fixing their silver lining. Ray's family home looked a bit like a big grey bubble with windows and doors. Weathervanes, sundials and other pointy contraptions protruded from the roof, and a shiny sign with the number nine on it poked out above the cloud.

Nim exploded just before landing, sending Ray hurtling into the freshly fixed silver lining and getting in a tangle.

'Aha!' said Cloudia as her daughter dangled like a spider's prey wrapped in the silvery threads. 'Nothing like arriving home in Ray Grey style, eh?'

Cloudia had lots of tools tucked into her messy mop of grey hair because she was always fixing or building things. Like her daughter, Cloudia had not one smidge of magic. But she was a fantastic cloud-architect and had even built their own house on Cloud Nine!

'How was school?' Cloudia asked as she attempted to unravel her daughter from the silver lining, using a plunger from her hair.

'We learned about some awful Rogues,' said Ray. 'And Mr Windbreaker told us about these mysterious Weatherlings who disappeared after Storm Tornadia!'

'Well, that sounds intriguing, do tell me more!' Cloudia said as she heaved her daughter up on to her lap. She ruffled Ray's hair and pulled her into a giant hug.

'They were called Rainbow Weatherlings!' said Ray. 'They used to be

SO powerful that they could stop Rogues, but then Tornadia Twist made them extinct.'

Cloudia looked impressed with Ray's knowledge. 'It sounds like we need those Rainbow Weatherlings more than ever. Your dad and the other Weather Warriors have been battling Storm Florence for over a week now.'

'Dad's never been away at a storm battle for this long before,' sighed Ray. 'I hope he's OK.'

Her mum pulled Ray a little closer. 'He'll be fine. Especially with Waldo by his side. I've never known a cloud-whale with such an attitude!'

'Waldo IS very grumpy!' chuckled Ray. Nim miaowed in agreement, farted, grew a cloud-beard and lost his tail. Then, to Ray's delight, a familiar voice shouted across the skies.

'OMELETTES!'

CHAPTER 5

AN A-RAY OF EARTHLY TREATS

'NO WAY!' cried Ray. 'It's Daaad!'

She waved her arms and jumped up and down as the bearded man wearing three ties approached, riding on the back of his cloud-whale, Waldo. Haze Grey was holding out his cloud-crook with one hand and had a basket of strange-looking things stashed behind him. As soon as her dad landed, he swept Ray up into a big hug and gave Cloudia a peck on the cheek.

'We've missed you so much, Dad!' said Ray, breathing in his dad-smell. His beard had got VERY spiky, but she didn't mind.

'I've been keeping up with Storm Florence every day on the Fizzogram,' said Cloudia. 'Sounds like you had to battle some of your worst Rogues yet!'

'Oh, there were some BEASTS!' said Haze.
'Quite literally. Florence Frozonia, the Snow
Rogue who orchestrated the whole storm, crafted
a hulking great snow-beast! It would try to SQUISH
us at any opportunity and used its sharp icy claws to
dig its way underground.' Haze shook his head.
'But luckily Waldo here gobbled the snow-beast
right up. Did I mention he was very hungry and
very grumpy?'

'Isn't Waldo ALWAYS very hungry and very
grumpy?!' laughed Cloudia.

Waldo grunted.

'Well, Dad, you're home just in time for the
Eclipse tonight!' sang Ray.

'It's tonight?!' gasped Haze. 'I'm so glad I'm
back, I wouldn't miss it for the world.Well . . . if
I happened to be called into work, then I'd probably
have to miss it for the world . . . Y'know, because
I'd need to help SAVE the world . . .'

'What are these?' interrupted Ray, poking at
the basket on Waldo's back.

'OH!' said Haze. 'How could I forget! As

always, every storm provides an A-RAY-RAY
of Earthly treats!'

Ray groaned at her dad's favourite joke.

'THIS is a basket of omelettes! For making
EGGS!' Haze paused, eyebrows furrowed. 'Or
was it the other way round . . .? ANYWAY, I
found them on the way home, scattered after a
small cow-nado swept through a farm in Oxford.'

Being a Weather Warrior meant that Haze
Grey spent many hours patrolling the skies and
keeping the Earth safe from Rogue storms.
But no matter how tired he was, he always made
time to bring Ray home any fascinating human
objects he'd found on his travels to add to her
collection.

'And THIS is called a *flip-flop*,' Haze
explained, slipping a strange object on to his ear.
'I think you wear it like this.' He struck a pose.
'As Storm Florence made its way to the coast of
India, I ended up fighting a terrible monsoon. Just
when I thought we'd lost the battle, this flip-flop
hit the ol' Rain Rogue Drizella on the head!'

Ray gave her dad a big hug. 'I love the flip-flop! Thank you!'

Haze also gave Ray a pumpkin – quite possibly the weirdest thing she had EVER seen – a pack of second-class stamps and a spotty shower cap.

While the family munched on their eggs for dinner (they were nice, if a little crunchy), Ray showed her mum and dad the book about rainbows she'd found in the school library. She plonked it on to the kitchen table creating a big puff of dust.

'Does that book actually have any pages left

in it?' asked Cloudia, peering at the tattered remains.

'Not many, but look!' Ray turned to the map and pointed to the big, fat cross next to *the Oldest Tree in the World*. 'Do you think that means treasure?' she asked.

Haze popped on a small pair of half-moon glasses and gazed at the map. 'A cross on a map USUALLY means treasure,' he said. He studied the old map a little closer and stroked his beard thoughtfully.

'I want to go and find it!' said Ray.

'Well, you can't leave the Weatherlands on your own until you're eighteen,' said Cloudia.

Ray blew a raspberry. 'Arrrgh, why can't I hurry up and be old already? Dad, can you take me to find the treasure one day? You know Earth inside out, so we wouldn't get lost!'

Haze's eyes lit up. He was about to answer when the pointer on the Compass Caller attached to his top pocket started to spin wildly, making a whirring sound. Haze flipped open the compass face, and a fizzling voice spoke.

'*Haze, it's Gale Miller 'ere. Look, I know you've probably JUST got home, and I know 'ow excited you were about your omleggs, but we 'ad another call-out. A Storm Helen is raging across the southern 'emisphere, paired with Storm Levison in the north. We've got fire wolves, lightning orbs and thunder louder than sonic booms with this one . . . We need you to come back to work . . .*'

Haze's cloud-whale Waldo did NOT look happy to be going back to work so soon. Haze looked at Ray sadly.

'I'm so sorry,' he said, then lifted Ray's chin gently. 'I promise you as soon as I get home we will go on an adventure together . . . and YOU can guide us to the treasure. JUST like that La Breeze you're so fond of.'

Ray smiled and gave her dad a big hug. 'It's La Blaze, but I'll forgive you this once,' she said with a wink. Then she gasped. 'Oh no! You're going to miss the Eclipse tonight!'

'I know.' Haze sighed. 'Luckily I've seen it a few times. But make sure YOU go and enjoy every second! It still can't believe the humans don't believe the Moon is made out of cheese!' He chuckled heartily and gave Ray a kiss on the head. 'Anyway, I best get going. You can tell me all about the Eclipse and we'll find that treasure when I'm back home again.'

CHAPTER 6

LA BLAZE

It was a few hours until midnight, and the Sunflower in the sky was shining brightly. It was time to set off for the Eclipse Festival! Ray had her rainbow book tucked in her bag, ready to show her friends the mystery cross.

Ray and her mum picked up Snowden on the way since his Forecaster parents were very busy making Canada all snowy, and his Granny Everfreeze was far too wobbly to go anywhere.

'I've got something really exciting to show you and Droplett!' Ray said to Snowden as Nim made a rather explosive landing in the gardens that surrounded the Sun Citadel.

'Oh?' said Snowden with a wonky smile. 'Can't you show me now? I won't tell Droplett.'

Ray shook her head and chuckled. 'You know Droplett will splosh me in the bum if she finds out I told you first!'

Tall sunflowers lined the Citadel grounds, which were decorated with beautiful bunting and mini sunflower garlands that sparkled in the sunlight. Food stands, umbrellas and games stalls lined up where the gardens met the surrounding Forest of Fahrenheits. At the very bottom of the pointy Citadel building was an open archway with a large flowerpot in its centre, and from this grew a thick Sunflower stem. The stem wound ALL the way to the roof of the Citadel, and at the very top was the big sunflower in the sky.

The Earth's SUN.

Five SunKeepers used their magic to keep the Sunflower glowing. It was a very important job being a SunKeeper, with the responsibility often passed down through sun families for generations.

Droplett arrived shortly after Ray, with Madame Trickle and the rest of the Weatherling orphans who lived at Trickle Towers. She skipped over to Ray with her arms full of bright blue cakes.

'LOOK! All of these cakes were free from the Rising Bun Bakery stand! And free stuff *always* tastes better, right?!' she said proudly. 'Apparently, they were an "unstable batch" – whatever THAT means – and they were about to be thrown away! Can you believe it?!'

'You do know what kind of cake that is, don't you, Droplett?' asked Ray, taking a wary step backwards.

'A tasty one?'

'They're rumblebuns!' said Ray, taking another step.

'Rum-bum-whats?!' said Droplett, looking confused. The buns suddenly began to shudder and shake in her grip. 'Oh! *What above Earth is happening?!*'

'If you don't eat them fast enough, they erupt!' said Ray.

'WHAT?'

A deep grumble emanated from the pile of cakes.

'Quick, guys. Eat them!' Droplett urged.

'We can't eat them ALL right now!' cried Snowden, hiding behind Ray.

Droplett looked from side to side. Then she swished her rain cape to swiftly summon a puddle, before throwing the whole armful of buns into the water with one great big PLOP!

Silence.

The friends stared at the puddle. It remained still. Thankfully.

'PHEW,' said Droplett. 'That was close!'

Before long, the palace gardens were PACKED with every kind of Weatherling, eating, dancing and having fun. There was still some time before the Eclipse. Ray was dying to tell her friends all about the map and the X marks the spot.

'Mum, can we go off by ourselves for a little

while?' she asked hopefully.

'As long as you don't leave the Citadel gardens,' said Cloudia. 'Let's meet back at the Weather Wobble stand for the Eclipse in an hour, OK? We can all watch it together!'

Ray and her friends headed into the hustle and bustle of the festival, making sure to eat as much free food as they could on the way.

'So, what's your exciting news, Ray?' asked Snowden.

'THIS!' said Ray, holding up *The Magic of Rainbows*.

Snowden and Droplett looked unimpressed.

'Ray, it doesn't look like there's much left of that book,' said Snowden as another half a page drifted to the floor.

Ray grimaced. 'I know. But I was looking for any books about the mysterious Rainbow Weatherlings in the school library, and this was the only thing I could find. But THIS was inside!' She opened the book to the last of the remaining pages showing the map and the cross.

'Oooooh! Treasure?' said Droplett, leaning in to get a better look.

Snowden's ears began pouring with think-flakes. 'Intriguing!' he muttered.

'A big cross on a map usually means treasure, right?' said Ray. 'Even my dad thinks it's treasure and he's a grown-up! Finding a mysterious treasure is every explorer's dream. And Dad said we can go find it together when he returns from his next big weather battle!'

'Now THAT'S exciting!' said Droplett. 'What do you think the treasure is?'

Ray shrugged. 'Maybe it has something to do with the lost Rainbow Weatherlings? It could be proof they existed!'

'If you found *actual* proof, then that would make you an instantly famous explorer for sure, Ray!' said Snowden with a wonky grin.

'I KNOW!' Ray was so excited at the thought, she felt as if she might erupt like a rumblebun.

As the friends approached the edge of the forest, Ray saw something that surprised her so much that she *did* erupt with a little fart. Because, tucked away into one of the few shadows of the garden, almost hidden behind a large pile of books and a pigeon reading a newspaper, was none other than –

'LA BLAZE DELIGHT!' Ray screamed. 'AND Coo La La!'

'La who-de-who and who-de-har?' asked Droplett.

'It's the explorer Ray loves,' said Snowden. 'And . . . a pigeon? With a top hat . . . and a monocle. I respect that guy.'

'AAAAAARGH! YES!' Ray shrieked. 'I had NO idea she'd be here signing books! Wobbling weathervanes, I can't believe it's ACTUALLY HER!'

La Blaze was at a small table piled high with all of her books. The Sun Weatherling was so beautiful. Her lemon hair shimmered and moved lightly in the air as if she were underwater. She was wearing a long waistcoat and two sunflowers on her wrists for channelling her sun magic.

'If La Blaze is a Sun Weatherling, why didn't she become a SunKeeper?' asked Snowden curiously.

Ray shrugged. 'I guess she decided to go her own way instead of following family tradition.'

'Why don't you talk to her?' suggested Droplett, nudging Ray forward. 'It's not like anyone else is queuing.'

Ray walked over to La Blaze's small table shyly and cleared her throat. Her heart was practically THUDDING out of her chest.

'YES?' the pigeon said sharply, ruffling his black and white speckled feathers and adjusting his monocle. 'Agent Coo La La here. You wish to speak to La Blaze? She is VERY busy. You may have to wait HOURS.'

Ray looked around the very empty surrounding area. Then Snowden sneezed, sending a stream of snowballs from his nostrils across La Blaze's table of books. Droplett put her head in her hands.

'I think I'm allergic to something around here,' Snowden sniffed, glancing at the pigeon.

La Blaze chuckled. 'Move aside, Coo La La, you're making the poor boy go all red in the face!' she said.

The pigeon gave Snowden an icy stare. The Sun Weatherling pushed her glasses to the end of her nose and offered her hand to Ray.

'How DeLIGHTful to meet you all!'

Ray stared at La Blaze's hand blankly.

Droplett nudged her in the ribs. 'You're being all weird and sunstruck, Ray. SPEAK.'

'I LOVE YOU!' Ray spluttered. 'I mean HELLO, LaLight! I mean, hi, Blaze Da La! I mean, BaLa Belight . . . howdy!'

Blushing furiously, Ray felt like her tongue was in a right tangle. But La Blaze chuckled kindly, making Ray feel completely at ease.

'This is Ray, your biggest fan in the sky!' said Droplett, patting her friend's shoulder.

'Well, kid, that's delightful to know!' said La Blaze, her eyes a little brighter than before. 'It's always wonderful to speak to aspiring young Earth Explorers. Cute cloud-cat by the way!'

Nim purred and blushed. 'This is Nim!' said Ray proudly.

'Ah, short for Nimbus?' asked La Blaze.

Ray chuckled and shook her head. 'Oh no, it's short for Nimothy!'

'Ah!' La Blaze raised an eyebrow, as an unimpressed Coo La La flew to perch on her shoulder.

Ray took a deep breath. 'Um, La Blaze, would you mind signing a book for me?' she asked.

'Of course, kid!' said the Sun Weatherling, picking up one of the books from the table. 'Which one would you like? It's buy one get ALL of the rest for free . . .' She gave a strained smile, then sighed.

'Oh, it's OK!' said Ray. 'I've already got ALL your books. I even got extras from the library today!' She rummaged through her bag. 'Hmmm, I must've left them at home, but I have this one . . . Could you sign it for me, please?'

She plonked *The Magic of Rainbows* on to the table. La Blaze pulled it towards her – and froze.

CHAPTER 7

BOOM AND SPLODGE

'Um . . . sorry it's not one of *your* books, and it's a bit tatty,' said Ray. 'But I'd love it if you could sign this map?' She opened it to the right page. 'Just under the cross? I'm going to go on an adventure just like you to find this treasure!'

La Blaze touched the cross. 'Where did you find this book?' she asked quietly.

'In the school library,' said Ray.

'It's so old, one sneeze might turn it to dust!' Droplett added.

But La Blaze didn't react. She was still staring at the book. 'Rainbows,' she muttered.

'Have you heard about Rainbow Weatherlings?' asked Ray. 'They used to be super powerful, but Storm Tornadia wiped them all out, over a thousand years ago!'

'Hmmm.' La Blaze was staring intently at the map. 'I have indeed heard of them. They do seem extraordinary. A little *too* extraordinary. I've always wondered how anyone can eliminate ANY weather magic at all. Surely that's *impossible*.'

'Who knows!' Ray said. 'But whoever this Tornadia Twist was, she sure sounded bad.'

'Bad, but *brilliant*,' muttered La Blaze. Ray frowned and La Blaze chuckled. 'Don't look so worried, kid. I agree, she was BAD. What I mean is, she made a *name* for herself. Not in the right way, of course. But at least nobody will forget who she is.'

La Blaze scribbled her

signature underneath the big cross on the map and smiled. 'Anyway, it's MUCH better to be known for something GOOD, eh?'

Ray nodded happily. 'Just like you!' she said.

La Blaze raised an eyebrow. 'Sure,' she said gently.

'Thank you for signing my book,' said Ray, hardly able to believe her luck. 'I really do love *everything* you do.'

'Well, at least someone does!' La Blaze erupted with laughter and waved a hand.

Ray took a deep breath and summoned up all her courage to finally say something she'd ALWAYS want to say to La Blaze. 'I was born without weather magic,' she blurted out. 'And it was you who inspired me to keep pursuing my dream, no matter what! Just like you did when you decided not to be a SunKeeper.'

La Blaze's expression was unreadable for a moment, but then she smiled softly. 'Well, I'm glad you feel that way, kid.' She tugged at the collar of her jacket and cleared her throat. 'Even now

I still have big dreams. And I'm determined
to make them come true . . . no matter what.'

Ray sat with her friends on a large log by the edge
of the forest, buzzing from her meeting with La
Blaze. Snowden unwrapped a very neatly packed
drizzle-pickle sandwich and Droplett gobbled up
at least seven lightning scones, covering her face
in skyberry jam.

Ray stared at the signature on the map. 'I still
can't believe I spoke to La Blaze! AND I have her
autograph.'

Droplett winked. 'We know, you've told us at
LEAST fifteen times already . . .'

'Sorry, I'm just SO happy!' said Ray. 'I hope
that when I become a brilliant Earth Explorer,
that maybe, just maybe, one day, I'll get to go on
adventure WITH La Blaze herself!' She touched
La Blaze's scribble lightly.

'You'll be travelling the Earth and skies, I'll be
TOP of the puddle-porting championships, and

Snowden will be making snowy weather all over the world!' said Droplett, fist-pumping the air.

'Sounds like we're going to be super busy Weatherlings when we grow up!' said Snowden wistfully.

'Well, we'll still have time to hang out,' said Ray. 'Promise we'll ALWAYS support each other no matter what?'

'PROMISE!' said Droplett, swooshing her cape and soaking Snowden's drizzle-pickle sandwich. He sighed as the sandwich slipped through his fingers and on to the floor, where it was immediately lapped up by a very happy Nim.

'I do promise! As long as you stop soaking my sandwiches,' said Snowden.

'Well well well. you all sound excited . . .'

'Makes us wonder why we weren't invited?!'

'Well, we WERE excited until you turned up,' grumbled Droplett.

Ray closed her book quickly as Frazzle and Fump marched over arm in arm, grinning nastily. Ray just knew that they weren't here for a nice chat.

'Haven't you two got anything better to do than earwig on our conversations?' asked Ray, feeling annoyed. Nim miaowed angrily, and his whiskers fell off.

'*Seems like you're all enjoying that book?!*' said Frazzle, pointing at the tattered cover in Ray's hands.

'*Why don't you give us a little look?!*' said Fump.

Ray didn't budge. 'I'd rather not,' she said.

Frazzle stepped forward and poked at the cover with the tip of her lightning stick, scorching a tiny hole in it.

'Hey! Don't do that!' said Ray, snatching the book away and getting to her feet. 'Just leave us alone!'

'*PAH! We all know this rainbow stuff ain't even*

TRUE,' sneered Frazzle.

'*And this book looks as messy and rubbish as YOU!*'

The twins cackled and jeered.

Droplett braced her rain cape. 'We said go away!' she hissed.

But the twins cackled even louder, clearly enjoying themselves.

'*You gonna SPLASH us with water, with a swish and a twirl?!*'

'*We're not scared of an orphan rain girl!*'

Ray saw the usual fierce spark in Droplett's eyes flicker.

Snowden cleared his throat and adjusted his

glasses. 'You're both being pains in the bottom,' he said to the twins calmly. 'So kindly bog off.'

'Frazzle, Fump, you should apologise to Droplett,' said Ray coldly.

Droplett was standing very still. Too still. It made Ray's heart hurt to see her friend looking so sad. The twins looked at each other and burst out laughing once more.

To Ray's surprise, Droplett glanced up at her, smiled and winked, before disappearing into a puddle of water with a SPLOSH. Seconds later she reappeared holding an armful of rumblebuns. She threw them towards the twins just as the blue cakes exploded with a huge . . .

SpLoDGe!

The rumblebuns erupted EVERYWHERE, covering the twins from head to toe in sticky, cakey, syrupy pink goo. Frazzle looked utterly furious. Fump licked his arm happily, before remembering to frown like his sister.

Frazzle pointed at Ray. *'This is YOUR fault!'*

'The final insult!' cried Fump, hitting his thunder drum with his fist.

The ground shook, making Ray drop her rainbow book. She went to pick it up, but Frazzle flicked her lightning stick and lifted the book in a crackling web of bright green electricity.

'Give it back!' Ray pleaded.

Frazzle guided the book into her own hand, using her lightning power to zap a hole in each of the few remaining pages, one by one. She turned over to reveal the page with the big cross and got ready to zap it again.

'STOP!' Ray cried. 'I need it to find the treasure!'

Frazzle and Fump's eyes lit up. Ray felt a sinking feeling in her tummy.

Now the Striker twins definitely wouldn't give her the precious book back.

'Well well well – TREASURE you say?'

'Why do YOU care about treasure, RAY GREEEY?'

Ray stood up tall and said, 'Because I'm going to be an Earth Explorer just like La Blaze DeLight.'

CHAPTER 8

NEVER INSULT MY CLOUD-CAT

Frazzle and Fump were quiet for a few moments. Then they burst out laughing and snorting, with the occasional laugh-induced fart from Fump. Frazzle pointed to where La Blaze was still perched at her table. She hadn't had one visitor since Ray.

'*HER? She's nothing special, I've not heard 'er name!*'

'*I guess you like 'er 'cause you're kinda the same.*'

'I believe in Ray,' said Snowden. 'She'll be the best Earth Explorer the Weatherlands has *ever* seen.'

But the twins weren't budging.

'*No way – an explorer?! We don't believe THAT!*'

'Not the WEATHERLESS girl and her REJECT cloud-cat!'

Ray's cheeks flushed but she still fired her glariest glare at Frazzle. 'I don't care what you say about ME, but NEVER insult my cloud-cat!' she snapped. Nim miaowed and then imploded. 'And weather magic or no weather magic, I WILL be an Earth Explorer!'

'We don't believe it, not one BIT!' sneered Frazzle, centimetres away from Ray's face. And Fump added, *'If I were YOU, I think I'd just QUIT!'*

The word 'QUIT' cut through Ray like an icicle. She might not have had any weather magic, and sure, her cloud-cat did explode, but ONE thing Ray Grey definitely didn't do, was QUIT.

'Fine,' said Ray in a steady voice. 'I'll prove it.'

Snowden shot Ray a worried look. 'Um, Ray? Prove what?'

Ray didn't take her eyes off Frazzle and Fump. 'I'll prove that I have what it takes to be an Earth Explorer.'

'Ray, you don't have to prove ANYTHING to those mean twins!' whispered Droplett.

Ray knew that, deep down. But the truth was, she wanted to prove it to herself.

'I'll get the treasure,' she said calmly. 'And I'll bring it back here to show you. TONIGHT.'

Frazzle and Fump, for once, were silent.

'Ray . . . it's FORBIDDEN to go to Earth unless you're with a grown-up!' said Snowden.

'Well,' said Ray, standing firm and thinking about her hero, just a few metres away. 'Sometimes explorers have to do things or go to places they're not meant to go. That's the only way they make discoveries and find the things nobody else finds. I'm going to Earth to find the treasure, and that's final!'

'But Ray, the Eclipse is in just under an hour,' said Snowden, his eyes full of concern. 'We won't see this again for another ELEVEN years! Also, your mum said not to leave the Citadel gardens!'

'And didn't you say you were going to find the treasure with your dad when he came home again anyway?' Droplett added. 'I'm all for breaking rules, but this is a BIT much.'

Ray felt a sudden pang of guilt, but she couldn't go back on her words now. 'I've made my decision, and I'm NO quitter!'

She scowled at Frazzle and Fump and started to walk towards the forest.

'RAY!' Snowden called out. 'Wait!'

But Ray walked on, hugging her rainbow book to her chest. She kept going until she reached the Weatherstone Circle, where she stopped and waited for her friends to catch up. Frazzle and Fump were trailing behind them, and Nim finally reappeared.

'I'll meet you guys back here,' said Ray. 'Frazzle, Fump, that means you too. You'll be wanting to see proof of the *treasure*, after all.'

Frazzle and Fump glanced at each other, then shrugged and folded their arms.

'Can we at least go with you?' asked Droplett. 'What if you cross paths with a Rogue?! You'll need someone to SPLOSH 'em!' She clenched her fists and boffed the air.

'Nobody should be leaving Celestia at all,' said Snowden. 'It's against the rules and it's DANGEROUS.'

'I know. But I'll be fine,' said Ray bravely. 'I can't be a Forecaster or a Weather Warrior or a Sky Academy teacher or anything that requires magic, but I can be an Earth Explorer! It's ALL I've ever wanted and I have to do this alone, just like La Blaze would!'

Snowden sighed. 'You're not going to back down, are you?' he said.

'You should know me well enough by now to know Ray Grey never backs down!' Ray turned to her cloud-cat and patted him between the ears. 'Ready for your biggest flight yet, Nim?'

Nim miaowed happily and expanded so that Ray could hop on to his back. She turned to her friends.

'I need you all to make me a promise,' she said.

'Not to tell ANYONE what I'm doing. OK?'

Droplett saluted. Snowden nodded sadly. Frazzle and Fump rolled their eyes.

'Ergh, fine, yes . . .'

'All right, I guess . . .'

'OK, Nim,' said Ray. 'No exploding if you can help it, please.'

Nim purred deeply and revved himself up. Then one very determined girl and her cloud-cat took to the skies, far away from the cheers and music coming from the Eclipse Festival below.

CHAPTER 9
DUCK-NADO

As Nim flew further and further away from the
Weatherlands, Ray didn't feel so brave any more.
But they kept on flying. She pulled out the small
compass that she always kept safely stashed in her
waistcoat pocket, and checked it against the map
in *The Magic of Rainbows* to make sure they were
heading the right way.

'Wow!' Ray gasped when she saw Earth in all
its glory. 'Isn't that just the most beautiful thing
you've ever seen, Nim?'

One half of the planet was lit up by the big
Sunflower in the sky. The other side, furthest
away, was steeped in darkness.

Ray spotted a Cloud Forecaster guiding a flock
of cloud-sheep across the skies, before they
morphed into speckled white floofs. 'Oooh,
look, Nim! I think she's doing an Altocumulus

cloud spell!' Ray had never actually seen Forecasters at work before. She'd only read about them in books at school.

Nim purred merrily and attempted to imitate the cloud-sheep, but ended up losing his whiskers.

Ray lowered herself into Nim's fluffy body as they passed a Rain Forecaster creating a light drizzle over a very grey-looking city in the north of England. If anyone spotted Ray flying through the Earth skies alone, they'd be sure to stop her.

As they flew over the North Pole, the sky became very busy with Snow Forecasters crafting delicate snow spells to create sparkly snowfall over the Arctic Circle.

Ray checked the map again. 'I think we're close, Nim!' she said. 'We just need to find the treasure and then get back home in time for the Eclipse.'

She realised she could no longer even see the Weatherlands. All she could see was the big Sunflower in the sky – and that didn't even look like a sunflower any more; it was just a big, glowing ball of yellow. Her heart was beginning to beat faster, the further from home she got.

'Come on, be brave!' Ray said to herself as she and Nim crossed countries speckled with trees and fields, and deserts and mountains, broken up by large expanses of ocean. Ray could hear the waves crashing against the rocks on the shore below. It was very soothing, and for a moment, Ray forgot all about feeling nervous.

'If La Blaze can climb the unclimbable mountain to search for the lost yeti treasures, or explore the seas looking for the mer-pire pearls, AND trek through dangerous forests searching for samples of unicorn poo, then I can make it to the Oldest Tree in the World and find this mystery treasure!' Ray fist-pumped the air. 'If I get back to the festival in time, I could even tell La Blaze about my DARING quest!'

She squinted at the map. It suddenly became rather difficult to see. The sky was getting darker, and not because of the time of day. This was a different kind of darkness. An ominous, suppressing darkness. The air felt thick and electric and the clouds grew dirty like a big bowl of grubby grey soup. This wasn't the kind of weather the Forecasters planned. This was the work of . . .

'Rogues,' Ray whispered as a shiver ran down her spine.

A blast of hot air hit her face, almost sending her flying. Ray gripped Nim's back, wincing as tiny prickles of searing heat speckled her cheeks. A flash of light made her jump, followed by the LOUDEST rumble of thunder Ray had ever heard. Nim miaowed and wibbled precariously.

'It's OK, Nim, let's keep flying!' said Ray, rubbing the cloud-cat between the ears.

The darkness was all-consuming now. As the lightning lit the whole sky, the dirty storm clouds swirled, full of red eyes, and spindly tornados weaved their way from the clouds to the ground like tentacles. Ray could hear cackles of laughter between the claps of thunder and felt the sweat trickling down her back. Nim gave another worried miaow. This was Ray's last chance to turn back.

'I've got this far. I can't back out now,' Ray said to herself. 'We're almost there, Nim! We can do this!'

Nim flew deeper into the storm. Ray was sure a Rogue would see her, but they seemed to be too busy partying in the murky skies.

'At least while they're distracted, I can find the treasure and get out of here!' said Ray.

But Ray had spoken too soon. Hailstones the size of ducks fell from above, almost knocking her off course. Then Ray realised they *were* in fact ducks, plummeting from the sky before getting caught up in a fierce whirlwind.

'QUUUUUUAAAAAAAAACK!' cried a desperate duck as it narrowly missed Ray's head.

'Oh no, Nim! It's a DUCK-NADO!' cried Ray, trying to steer them out of the quacking disaster. She knew about Wind Rogues and their tormenting tornadoes. Her dad had told her ALL about the The New York SHOE-NADO of 1962 (the high heels were lethal). And then there was the Australian Knicker-nado of 1988 . . . but the less said about THAT, the better.

Ray flew Nim away from the dizzying duck-nado as fast as she could, disorientated by the deafening quacks and the frantic flapping of wings. They headed towards a quiet spot on solid ground, and for the first time EVER, Nim landed WITHOUT exploding.

'Well done, Nim!' Ray cheered, before realising the cloud-cat's face was missing.

'Wobbling windsocks!' said Ray, clutching her chest. But Nim miaowed and Ray saw that his face was on his belly.

'This is the moment of truth,' said Ray. 'I'm about to touch the EARTH for the FIRST time!'

She slid off Nim's back with a light thump, and squeaked happily.

'It feels EARTHY!' She chuckled, kicking at the dirt. 'I expected more green really.' Then she looked up. Her heart sank. The whole place was completely submerged in a thick fog.

'That's a shame,' she said, squinting to get a better look. But the fog was too thick, and Ray started to feel uneasy.

'This place feels lonely,' she said quietly as she tiptoed through the hazy blanket with Nim close by her side. She pulled out her trusty compass again, and checked the map. 'Well, Nim, I think the Oldest Tree should be right HERE!'

Something large and dark loomed out of the mist.

'That must be it!' Ray gasped.

But as she stepped closer and the mist parted, she saw that this tree – which was bigger than ANY tree Ray had ever seen – was completely dead. Petrified, burnt and smashed to smithereens, this tree looked like it had been through the worst storm ever.

Ray had seen pictures of the Rogues' work in her school textbooks. But seeing the result up close overwhelmed her with sadness.

'Why would anyone want to do this to a tree! You poor thing.' She leaned forward to touch its trunk lightly. There was a flash of bright green light then a BOOM!

'Yikes! What was that?' shrieked Ray as the ground shook.

Nim exploded in fright. Another bright light flashed, and two figures appeared, silhouetted in the fog ahead of Ray. One was wide with HUGE fists and the other tall and skinny . . .

Thunder 'n' Lightning Rogues!

Nim's floofy body was slowly reassembling in all the wrong places, with his eyes on his bum and his bum on his nose. He was in no fit state for a quick escape. In the nick of time, Ray squeezed herself into a gap in the dead trunk just as the Thunder 'n' Lightning Rogues arrived at the tree.

'EY!' one of the Rogues cried. 'DID YOU SEE SUMMIN', BLAP?'

'Nah, Bop, you need ter get yerself some glasses, I keep tellin' ya!'

Ray wedged herself a little further into the hollow trunk, but the ground beneath her feet gave way and she went tumbling down, down, down into the roots of the tree.

Holding on tightly to a large root, Ray let her eyes adjust to the darkness. 'Nim? Nim! Are you OK?! Where are you?' she whispered.

Nim appeared with a light POOF next to her and nuzzled into Ray's neck.

'I'd love to be affectionate right now, but I'm dangling by a ROOT in a big black pit,' said Ray, holding on for dear life.

Something caught her eye. A tiny beacon of multicoloured light in the centre of the pit, seemingly suspended in mid-air.

'Nim, do you think you could fly me to that glowy thing?' Ray said with excitement. 'That must be the buried treasure!'

Nim expanded enough so that Ray could carefully slip on to the safety of his floofy back.

'Now PLEASE don't explode, we have no idea how deep this goes!' she said.

She slowly guided the cloud-cat over to the strange light.

'Wow!' said Ray breathlessly. The light was tiny wisps of colour swirling around inside what looked like a black crystal. 'TREASURE!' Ray gasped, and reached for the glowing object.

Her palm tingled. The black crystal felt warm.

Ray watched the colours swirling around inside, like a sparkly liquid magic eager to get out. What was it? La Blaze would know. She had to show it to her!

Ray slipped the crystal carefully inside her waistcoat pocket and looked up. 'We need to get out of here, Nim,' she said quietly. She could just make out the voices of the Thunder 'n' Lightning Rogues up above. She'd have to wait until they'd gone.

Ray was suddenly becoming VERY aware of the time. She had to make it back to the Sun Citadel before the Eclipse, otherwise her mum would be worried about her. Not to mention that Ray would be in a LOT of trouble for travelling to Earth all by herself!

After what felt like an eternity, Ray finally heard a sizzle and a crack and a rumble, and then it was silent.

Ray swung herself on to Nim's back and they emerged from the gap of the tree trunk into the stormy landscape. The Rogues continued to party hard in the swirling storm above, and it was now raining so heavily that the ground was flooding fast. On the plus side, the ducks from the duck-nado were now happily swimming in the expanding lake of water.

Take-off was rather tricky with the rain smashing against her cheeks, but Ray guided Nim as best she could whilst trying not to fall off. Finally, the rain eased, the murky skies parted, and the sun shone once again.

'Phew,' said Ray as the Weatherlands fizzled back into view. 'We did it! And it's still light, which means the Eclipse hasn't started yet!'

CHAPTER 10

THE ECLIPSE

Ray was greeted by a faceful of rain and snow when she arrived bottom first in the Weatherstone Circle. Snowden and Droplett threw their arms around their friend and squeezed her tight.

'We were getting worried!' said Snowden. 'The Eclipse is starting any minute now! We weren't sure you were going to make it in time!'

'I'm here, I'm here!' said Ray, feeling relieved and rubbing her sore bottom. 'GUYS! Earth is AMAZING! The sea is SO much bigger than it looks in our schoolbooks, and it's so weird seeing the light and dark side!'

'What was the Oldest Tree in the World like?' asked Droplett, bouncing from one foot to the other.

'It's MASSIVE!' Ray sighed. 'And dead.'

'Oh . . .' said Droplett and Snowden at the same time.

'*WELL, I see no treasure? Did you even go?*'

'*Or are you just putting on a show?!*' Frazzle and Fump chorused.

Ray puffed out her chest. Then she reached inside her waistcoat pocket to pull out the big black crystal. The colourful wisps were still furiously swirling around inside.

'WOW!' said Droplett. 'Now THAT is what I call *treasure*!'

'What *is* it?' asked Snowden as think-flakes poured from his nostrils.

'Some kind of crystal,' said Ray. 'I've read about lots of crystals in some of La Blaze's books. But I've never read about anything like this one.'

'Those swirly bits inside look so pretty!' cooed Droplett. Her nose was pressed up against the treasure crystal.

'I'm going to go show it to La Blaze! I hope she's still at the festival,' Ray said, hardly able to contain her excitement. 'I can't wait to see her face when she sees it!'

'*We should take the treasure, we encouraged*

you to go.'

'*Frazzle is right, we deserve it you know!*'
sang the twins.

'No way!' Ray replied with a frown. 'You didn't
encourage me. You were really mean to me. I was
the one who CHOSE to go. And now I've proven
that I am a proper Earth Explorer just like La
Blaze!'

Frazzle and Fump scowled and marched
towards Ray.

'*Stop making a fuss.*'

'*Just give it to US!*' Frazzle held out her
lightning stick.

Droplett growled and brandished her rain
cape. Ray stood firm, holding the black crystal
close to her chest.

Around them, the shadows of the
Weatherstones slowly disappeared.

'The Eclipse! It's starting!' cried Droplett.

The sunlight dimmed. Lots and lots of tiny
sparkles filled the darkening sky.

'Stars!' Ray whispered.

The Moon King appeared high above holding his large plate of round cheese – the Earth's Moon. He began a merry dance with the stars in the night sky.

Ray gasped. 'I told Mum we'd watch the Eclipse together! We'd better head back –'

But then there was an almighty CRACK. The crystal in Ray's hands burst open, the wisps of magic escaping. Ray yelped and dropped it.

'Snowden, Droplett! Are you seeing this?!' she squeaked.

The wisps sparkled and shifted from reds to oranges and yellows, to greens, bright blues, to darker blues and vibrant purples.

'Sizzling snowflakes!' gasped Snowden.

'Ray!' cried Droplett. 'What's happening?'

The ground beneath Ray's feet began to shudder. There was a deep grumbling sound. Snowden and Droplett stumbled backwards, falling on to their bottoms as the Striker twins watched on in horror.

The crystal became smaller and smaller, melting away. More colourful wisps escaped, until the black crystal disappeared completely; all that was left were the colours hovering in the air, which began to swirl around Ray.

'Ray, whats happening?!' said Droplett, trying to keep her balance as the ground shook violently.

Snowden grabbed Droplett's hand and reached out to Ray. 'Let's get out of here!'

The colours were still swirling around Ray like a colourful blanket, and her friends' voices became distant.

'RAAAAAAY!'

'It's eating her up!'

Ray felt a warm tingle of energy flow through her. She tried to call out, but she couldn't speak. She tried to move, but she was frozen. Ray tried to blink, but her eyes were transfixed. She felt her feet leave the ground – saw large sparkling snowflakes swirling around her with huge drops of rain. Wind was rushing through her hair and lightning crackled from her fingertips. She felt different. Invincible.

With one almighty BOOM, beams of multicoloured light burst from the centre of the Weatherstone Circle. The six Weatherstones began to glow in turn. Sun, snow, rain, cloud, wind, thunder 'n' lightning . . .

Ray was still rising, surrounded by all the different types of weather, all the beautiful colours. She felt . . . POWERFUL.

But then, as the Eclipse came to an end and a sliver of sunlight stretched across the stone circle, all the strange feelings disappeared.

Ray felt herself falling.

'Ray?'

'RAY?!'

'IS SHE DEAD?'

'Calm down, Droplett, she's not dead . . .' Ray felt something poke her forehead. 'Well, maybe she's a *tiny* bit dead.'

Ray slowly woke up. Her view was filled with two beady eyes, and a tiny mouth with a beard.

'Miaow?'

'Nim!' Ray said weakly, scooping him into a big hug.

Snowden took Ray's hand and helped her up.

Ray furrowed her eyebrows, trying to work out why she'd been lying on the ground. 'Is the Eclipse over?' she said.

'The Eclipse is NOT the point right now, Ray! Don't you remember *what JUST HAPPENED*?' said Droplett.

Ray's head felt all spinny and WEIRD. 'Not really. I . . . did I faint?'

'You didn't exactly *faint* . . .' said Snowden. He gulped and adjusted his glasses. Ray could tell he had something he wanted to say. But then Frazzle and Fump bodged their way in, almost knocking the poor boy to the floor.

'*Your hair is all colourful! HOW?! WHY?!*'

'*AND how above Earth did you just fly!*'

'Fly?' Ray said. 'And what do you mean my hair is all *colourful*?'

Droplett swished her cape, creating a puddle on the ground. 'Maybe it's better if you see for yourself,' she said.

Feeling a bit wobbly, Ray leaned over Droplett's puddle to look at her reflection.

'Wobbling weathervanes,' she whispered, when she saw the girl looking back at her.

The girl in the reflection didn't have short grey hair.

THIS girl had very long hair. And it was full of bright COLOURS – from red, orange, yellow and green, to blue, indigo and violet!

CHAPTER 11

FLIPPIN' FOGHORNS

Ray blinked hard, rubbed her eyes, then peered into the puddle again. Her hair was still very much multicoloured.

'Um . . . it suits you?' said Droplett.

'I . . . I . . .' Ray stuttered. Then she gasped, remembering the picture on the front of *The Magic of Rainbows* book. She pulled it out from her bag and stared at the faded cover illustration. 'My hair looks JUST like this Weatherling's hair! Look! The colours are exactly the same!' She held up the book to show her friends. She didn't know what to say or how to process what was happening.

'Well, that's odd because that's a picture of a Rainbow Weatherling!' said Droplett with a frown.

'What was *in* that treasure crystal?!'

spluttered Ray, looking around for the black gem.

'The crystal is very much gone,' said Snowden. 'It kind of melted away when all the colours burst out of it. And whatever those colours were, they now seem to be inside YOU, Ray,' he added, his eyes wide as a stream of think-flakes floated out from his left nostril.

Ray let out a long whistle.

'Oh, and whilst you were floating with colours swirling around you, an extra Weatherstone burst from the ground!' Droplett added. She pointed to the centre of the stone circle.

Ray looked over at the new Weatherstone. Nim was circling it to find the ultimate spot in the sunlight. She was about to check out this new standing stone when Frazzle and Fump blocked her way.

'I'd forgotten you were here,' sighed Ray.

Frazzle pulled out her lightning stick and pointed it at Ray threateningly. Tiny sizzles of bright green electricity popped out from the end.

What did you DO, 'she hissed.

'*We don't trust YOU!*' Fump growled, close behind his sister.

'I didn't DO anything! Not on purpose anyway,' said Ray defensively. 'You were there the whole time, you *saw* what happened! I was holding the treasure crystal and the colours burst out of it and – well, now I have colourful hair!'

Frazzle flicked her lightning stick at the rainbow book still in Ray's grip. Sparks flew as the remaining pages fizzled into a sizzling green ash. Then Fump hit his thunder drum, creating a MIGHTY rumble. The twins poked their tongues out and began to walk off.

'They're NOT getting away with that!' growled Droplett.

'To be honest, I'd rather they just left us alone,' said Ray, gathering up the ruined book and stuffing it back in her bag.

But Droplett was already marching up behind the twins. The tiny Rain Weatherling swished her rain cape and a huge torrent of water SPLOSHED Frazzle and Fump from head to toe.

The twins turned slowly, dripping with rainwater. Droplett spun back towards Ray with a big smirk plastered across her face.

'That'll show them!' she said with a wink.

Then two things happened next. And they happened VERY fast.

Eyes flashing, Frazzle flicked her lightning stick, sending a sharp bolt of green electricity crackling and spinning towards Droplett's bottom.

'DROPLETT! Behind you!' shrieked Ray, holding her hands out.

Flashes of red, orange and yellow whizzed through Ray's mind. Then green, blue, indigo and violet.

A surge of prickling energy flooded through her

whole body and out through her fingertips. The next thing Ray knew, the colours were pouring from her outstretched hands, all the way to the lightning bolt. The zigzag beam of bright green electricity was now caught in mid-air, crackling angrily, centimetres away from Droplett's bottom.

Frazzle frowned and flicked her lightning stick again. Nothing happened.

That's when Ray realised that the prickling energy didn't belong to her.

'I have control of Frazzle's lightning bolt!' she yelped.

'*WHAT*?!' cried Frazzle.

'*You do NOT!*' shouted Fump.

Frazzle flicked her lightning stick and again – nothing.

Rainbow colours streamed from Ray's hands, holding the lightning in place. Among the prickles and sizzles and the buzz of power, Ray felt a rush of panic overwhelm her. She didn't know what to do.

Ray kept as still as possible, trying to hold on to this POWER. Somehow, she knew that her grip on the lightning bolt was weakening.

'Droplett! MOVE!' she shouted.

Droplett grabbed the edges of her rain cape and disappeared into a puddle – just as the lightning bolt sizzled into the spot where her bottom had been just a few seconds earlier.

Droplett re-emerged next to Ray with a splosh.

There was silence. Fump looked a little scared. Frazzle shook Fump's shoulder, then grabbed him by the elbow, before they both retreated into the forest, out of sight.

'Did . . .' Ray began in a wobbly voice. 'Did colours just come out of my hands?'

The think-flakes were whizzing around Snowden's head so fast that you could hardly see his face. This meant his brain was on overload.

'They did,' he said slowly.

'Flippin' foghorns,' said Droplett, before spending the next two minutes puddle-porting around the Weatherstone Circle. She finally stopped directly in front of Ray and gripped both of her shoulders. 'THAT WAS THE WEIRDEST AND MOST AWESOME THING I'VE EVER SEEN! What kind of weather power was that?'

'I *think* . . .' Ray hesitated. She pulled out what was left of *The Magic of Rainbows* book from her bag, and stared at the faded band of colours stretching across the cover. The very same colours *she* had created with her hands.

'It can't be,' she muttered. 'It looks like rainbow weather magic. . .'

CHAPTER 12

ABSOLUTELY NOTHING UNUSUAL HAPPENED

'Rainbow weather magic?' said Droplett and Snowden at the same time.

'But I didn't think that existed any more,' added Droplett.

'Well, what else could it be? And now it's inside ME,' shrieked Ray.

Snowden shook his head. 'And what was it doing inside the crystal before that?' He was pacing back and forth. Think-flakes were pouring out of his ears and nostrils at an alarming rate. 'Even my Snow-It-All Mode can't work this one out. I can't believe there's something I don't know!'

Ray opened the sizzled pages of the rainbow

book to the Earth map, which had been ripped in half by Frazzle's lightning magic.

Droplett pointed to the cross. 'Someone must have known the treasure crystal was buried under the Oldest Tree in the World. Otherwise why would they have marked the map with a big cross?' she said suspiciously. 'I wonder if they KNEW that it contained rainbow weather magic?'

'Who would bury it anyway?' asked Ray.

The friends all gasped, before saying at the same time: 'A ROGUE!'

'Although this still doesn't explain why the magic went into ME!' said Ray.

'RAY?! Raaaaaaaaay?' cried a voice. 'Raaaaaaaay!'

'Uh-oh! That's Mum!' said Ray. She grabbed her colourful locks of hair. 'I can't let her see me like THIS!'

Snowden sprang to action, drawing a snowflake in the air. Just in the nick of time, Ray was wearing a tall and dashing snow wig.

Cloudia emerged from the woods looking flustered. 'Oh, Ray! KIDS. Thank the skies you're OK!'

'ABSOLUTELY NOTHING UNUSUAL HAPPENED!' Droplett yelled.

Snowden shot Droplett a disapproving look. Ray felt a lump of snow fall down the back of her neck.

'I was SO worried about you when you didn't turn up to watch the Eclipse!' said Cloudia. ' What were you thinking, leaving the Citadel gardens?'

PLOP.

Another lump of snow fell from Ray's head, and a long lock of bright red hair fell across her face. Cloudia gasped.

'Um, Mum?' said Ray quietly. 'There's something I need to tell you.'

'You see, Frazzle and Fump didn't think I had what it took to find the treasure. I wanted to prove them wrong!' Ray finished. She felt better now she'd told her mum everything.

'Ray, you should NOT have gone to Earth on your own!' said Cloudia, pacing around the Weatherstone Circle. 'And you don't need to prove yourself to ANYONE, *especially* not Frazzle and Fump Striker!'

'I also wanted to prove I had what it takes to be an explorer,' Ray admitted. Her shoulders slumped. 'I'm sorry, Mum, I really am.'

Cloudia's stern face softened. She placed both hands on Ray's shoulders. 'I'm just relieved you came back in one piece,' she said. 'Even if you DID come back with a few *extras*!'

'What do I do, Mum?' asked Ray. She figured mums always knew what to do. 'Do YOU think this is ancient rainbow weather magic?'

Cloudia put her hands on her hips. 'I'm no expert on magic as you know. But it's definitely not any magic I've seen.'

'Guys!' said Snowden suddenly. He was standing next to the new standing stone that

had appeared in the centre of the Weatherstone
Circle.

Cloudia tilted her head. '*That* Weatherstone
wasn't always there, was it?' she asked, walking
over to the stone with Ray and Droplett.

'No,' said Ray. 'It burst out of the ground
when I was floating and the strange magic went
inside me.'

The new standing stone looked just like
the other Weatherstones that circled
the clearing, but much bigger.
And just like the other
stones, there was a
symbol carved
into its front.

'That doesn't
look like any of the
other weather
symbols,'
said Ray,
studying the
carving.

'That stripy bit looks like the rainbow you made,' said Droplett, pointing to the stack of curved lines at the top.

Beneath the rainbow symbol was a long line with two circles at the top, and wings protruding from either side.

'That must be the rainbow instrument for channelling the magic,' said Ray. 'Like your rain cape, or Snowden's snow gloves . . .'

'Yeah, but what IS it?' asked Droplett. 'A pair of flying glasses stuck to a magic stick, maybe?'

'I'm sure I've seen it somewhere before,' said Ray. The rainbow instrument symbol was oddly familiar, but she couldn't work out why.

And she knew she hadn't seen it in her rainbow book, which was now completely sizzled and ripped to shreds. Ray sighed at the sight of it. 'I'm not sure this is going to be much use any more. It was already hanging together by a thread when I found it in the library. Now thanks to Frazzle, it's as good as a snowman in summer!'

'Kids, it's getting very late, and your guardians will be wondering where you are if I don't escort you home soon,' said Cloudia, 'And Ray? I think we need to digest ALL OF THIS,' she waved her arms around in a big circle, 'and then we must go and talk to the head of the Council of Forecasters first thing tomorrow.'

Ray gulped and nodded. 'OK, Mum,' she said. 'Can Snowden and Droplett come with us? They can help describe exactly what happened. Pleeeease?'

'I guess it would make sense,' Cloudia said, looking a little worried.

'We'll be there to eat breakfast with you FIRST thing in the morning!' cheered Droplett. 'Your mum's pitter-patter pancakes are WAY nicer than the sunset porridge they give us Trickle Towers!' She grinned at Cloudia.

Snowden agreed. 'Precisely. And pancakes or not, we made a promise to support each other – NO matter what!'

CHAPTER 13
THOSE THUNDERBUM-FACES

After taking Snowden and Droplett home, Nim flew Ray and her mum towards their home in the Cloudimulus Suburbs. But Cloud Nine was nowhere to be seen, because it was completely surrounded by Weatherlings with large notepads and Fog-Flashers.

'Are we expecting guests?' asked Ray, squinting to get a better look.

'They're not guests,' said Cloudia slowly. 'They're weather reporters!'

'Why would a bunch of reporters be gathering outside our house?' asked Ray.

'THERE SHE IS!'

'RAY GREY!'

All the reporters turned to look at the

approaching cloud-cat. They rushed over on wind instruments or skidded along waves of water to get to Ray first.

'*Ray Grey! Can you tell us what happened when you went to Earth?*'

'*Is it true you can make colours come from your hands?*'

The news was out already? HOW? thought Ray.

'Please get away from our house and leave my daughter alone!' Cloudia shouted crossly.

Ray struggled to keep her eyes open from all the Fog-Flasher flashes.

'*Frazzle and Fump Striker told us about your MAGICAL CRYSTAL TREASURE?!*'

'Those thunderbum-faces!' growled Ray. 'Why can't they just mind their own business?'

'*How did you acquire this weather magic?*'

'*Ray Grey! Is it true?! Did you try to attack Frazzle using HER OWN magic?*' asked a wind-reporter riding on a wind horn like a witch would ride a broom.

'I didn't attack anyone!' said Ray, shocked by

this accusation. 'Frazzle tried to zap my friend's bottom with her lightning weather magic, and then –'

Her mum cut in. 'Ray doesn't have to explain anything to you lot. Now fog off!'

More reporters arrived, surfing on slabs of snow or glowing sunflower skates. Cloudy puffs filled the air as they tried to take fogographs of Ray from every angle.

'*What does the new weatherstone MEAN?!*' asked a posh reporter on a cloud-platypus.

'*What did you have for dinner?*'

'*Where did I leave my glasses?*'

'Please move!' Ray's mum shouted sternly. 'This is none of your business!'

'*It's EVERYONE'S business,*' said another voice. '*Surely you should be more concerned by your daughter's mysterious powers?*'

'*Is she working for the Rogues?*'

'*Are YOU working for the Rogues?*'

The questions kept coming as more and more weather reporters snapped their Fog-Flashers.

Poor Nim was getting agitated. At least two reporters were tangled in Cloud Nine's silver lining. That's when Cloudia Grey lost it.

'THAT'S THE FIFTEENTH TIME I'VE FIXED THE SILVER LINING THIS WEEK, SO BACK OFF!' she bellowed, followed by some very naughty words.

Ray's heart began to beat faster. She really wished all of these reporters would just leave!

'*Ray, why are you refusing to talk to us?*'

'*Are you hiding something?!*'

Tingles started to flare up inside of her. Colours flashed through her mind and her head felt warm.

'*Ray Grey?!*'

So many feelings were throbbing through her.

'*Ray*! *Why are ignoring us*?!'

'*RAAAAAY*!'

'*RAAAAAAAAAY?!*'

Ray closed her eyes and clenched her fists tightly. An energy pulsed through her, the same energy she'd felt before taking hold of Frazzle's magic. There were GASPS. When Ray opened her eyes again, rainbow colours were pouring from her whole body: bands of red, orange, yellow, green, blue, indigo and violet. The reporters hung on to Cloud Nine's silver lining for dear life, or sprawled across the rooftop as they lost control of their weather magic. Because now EVERYONE'S magic was in RAY'S CONTROL.

Ray could feel the rushing wind, the electric lightning and rumbly ROARS of thunder. She had control of it ALL.

Cloudia gazed at Ray with wide eyes as the

colours splurged through the air. Raindrops began to swirl, and wind howled. Snowflakes danced around and the cloud-creatures floated helplessly among the swirling weather.

The reporters floundered, unable to understand why they couldn't use their own magic.

'*What's going on*?!' someone shouted.

'*Look! Ray's doing it! She's making the colours!*'

'*She's the one in control of our magic!*'

'*This is a MIRACLE!*'

'*No, it's a CURSE!*'

Ray saw a flicker of fear in her mum's eyes. All at once, the colours disappeared and Ray lost her grip on everyone's power – letting it go with an almighty SPLOSH and SPLODGE, a *WHOOOOOOSH* then a ZZZZZZZAP, followed by a BOOM and multiple POOFS as all the cloud-creatures exploded.

The rain died down, the snow fizzled away, the lighting faded, and the thunder was silenced. Finally, the reporters fled, not before sneaking in one last fogograph.

'Well,' said Cloudia as the last of the reporters flew away. 'Your father is certainly in for a BIG surprise when he returns home.'

'I . . . I'm sorry, Mum,' said Ray. 'I don't know how to control this new power . . . I . . . I . . .'

To Ray's relief, her mum smiled and put an arm around her tightly. 'You have nothing to be sorry for,' she said. 'And quite honestly? THAT was amazing.'

CHAPTER 14

I KNEW I'D SEEN IT BEFORE!

Ray could hardly keep her eyes open. She attempted to pour her cereal into her slippers and had somehow put on three pairs of knickers. She hadn't slept very well at all. So many questions had been swirling around her mind. WHY had ancient rainbow weather magic been inside that crystal she found? Who had buried it? Why had *she* gained this magic?

Ray was relieved to be back in the comfort of her own home, among her cloudy plants and collection of human objects, where everything felt ALMOST normal again. But when she saw the family pictures of herself with short grey hair, her tummy did a nervous roly-poly. What would happen when she went back to school on Monday? Would the other Weatherlings accept her?

How would the Council of Forecasters react?

Ray was so lost in her thoughts, she didn't realise she was still pouring the muggy milk on to her slipper-ful of frostbite flakes. The milk spilled off the edge of the table into Nim's open mouth.

'Stop worrying, Ray-Ray,' said Cloudia softly. 'Everything will be OK. The head of the Council of Forecasters will be able to help you. I promise.'

Snowden and Droplett arrived just in time for some freshly made pitter-patter pancakes. Whilst they munched away, Ray updated her friends on the reporter incident and how she'd used her rainbow weather magic on *everyone*.

'Wow!' said Droplett. 'How did it feel?'

'Overwhelming,' said Ray. 'I could feel all the different types of weather, but I didn't know what to DO with it! Or how to control it. It was a bit scary actually. I'm just glad I didn't hurt anyone.'

'Well, it's definitely not a secret any more,' said Snowden as the *Weekly Weathervane* newspaper blew in through the window courtesy of Postman Puff.

The front cover of the newspaper had the biggest and most unflattering picture of Ray, mid-blink and mid-speech, colour radiating from her whole body and hair, looking as if she'd been electrocuted.

'That is not your best look, Ray,' said Droplett, not even bothering to hide her giggles.

IS SHE A DANGER OR A SAVIOUR?

RAY GREY FINDS MYSTERIOUS CRYSTAL ON EARTH AND GAINS WEATHER POWERS THOUGHT TO HAVE BEEN LOST OVER A THOUSAND YEARS AGO. WHAT DOES THIS MEAN? REPORTERS SAY THE YOUNG WEATHERLING USED HER POWER TO TAKE CONTROL OF THEIR WEATHER MAGIC, RENDERING THEM DEFENCELESS.

'SHE LOOKED SO ANGRY,' SAID ONE CLOUD-REPORTER. 'AND THEN SHE MADE MY CLOUD-PLATYPUS EXPLODE. HE RE-FORMED WITH ONE EYE MISSING. RICHARD WILL NEVER BE THE SAME!' WEATHERLINGS ARE URGED TO STEER CLEAR OF RAY GREY IF YOU SEE HER.

'That is absolute FOGSWALLOP!' said Cloudia, poking at the newspaper page.

'They've made me sound like a villain,' said Ray sadly. 'I didn't mean to do any of that.'

'I'm going to call the head of the Council of Forecasters RIGHT now and sort out this mess!' said Cloudia angrily. 'Kids, go up to Ray's room and stay there. I'll be using some words you shouldn't be hearing.'

Ray, Snowden and Droplett headed up to Ray's bedroom. The walls were covered in drawings of Ray and her friends dressed as explorers on various adventures. And where there weren't drawings, there were posters of La Blaze, or cutouts from her books.

'What now?' asked Droplett, biting her lip.

Snowden shrugged as think-flakes poured from his ears.

'I can't believe this is happening!' cried Ray, slumping on to her bed. Nim sat on her head in an attempt to comfort her. 'I don't know how to CONTROL this magic . . .' Ray's voice was muffled beneath the cloud-cat's bum. 'What if I never get the hang of it?!'

'Well, like any Weatherling, you need a weather instrument to channel the magic,' said Snowden.

'The flying glasses on a stick we saw on the Rainbow Weatherstone, right?' asked Droplett. 'Where do you think we can find one?'

Ray sat up quickly, and Nim exploded. 'I KNOW I've seen that weather instrument before . . .' She wracked her brains. 'But WHERE?' She looked at her bookshelf. 'Maybe it's in one of my treasure books. Quick! Help me look!'

The friends pulled out book upon book (mostly La Blaze's adventures and the treasures she'd found) and sped through the pages, looking for any useful information. An hour went by and the friends had almost finished checking through EVERY book in Ray's room. Just as they were ready to admit defeat, Droplett swished her cape, sending a splosh of water over Snowden's head.

'Guys!' she said. 'Look!' Droplett was holding a book called *The Britolian Museum and its Finest Artefacts*. Ray and a rather damp Snowden rushed to her side and gasped.

'I knew I'd seen it before!' said Ray. 'I've pored over the treasures in this book a windillion and one times!'

There on the page was a photograph of a long golden staff with two rings at the top and two shiny wings at each side, titled 'MYSTERIOUS ANCIENT TREASURES DATING BACK TO THE DARK AGES'.

Ray's purple and blue eyes flashed with excitement. 'This looks JUST like the symbol carved into the Rainbow Weatherstone!'

'No doubt about it!' said Snowden with a grin.

'Well,' said Ray, getting to her feet. 'If I'M a Rainbow Weatherling, then I'll need my instrument. I have to go find it!'

'WOO HOO!' cheered Droplett. She turned to look at the book cover. 'But Ray . . . where's this Britolean Museum?'

Ray bit her lip and said quietly. 'On Earth . . .'

CHAPTER 15

THE BRITOLIAN MUSEUM

'There's no way you can go to Earth on your own AGAIN,' said Snowden, shaking his head. 'It's way too risky, especially now that everyone knows about you!'

'But NOT using a weather instrument to cast weather magic is against the rules,' replied Ray. 'And you've seen the chaos I cause at the moment.'

Snowden opened his mouth to speak, then paused. Ray was right.

'I'm more than happy to keep you company if you want to go find your weather instrument, Ray,' said Droplett, bouncing up and down on the bed. 'It'll be like out first REAL adventure as the explorer gang you're always drawing.' She pointed to Ray's pictures plastered to the walls. Snowden was quiet.

'Snowden, Weatherlings already think I'm dangerous,' said Ray. 'I need this instrument to control my magic. I almost lost control last night when all those reporters were surrounding me. If I have the instrument, then I can learn to use this magic properly. I don't want to be a danger to my friends and family. I could never, ever live with myself if anything bad happened to any of you.'

Ray felt a cold hand takes hers. 'OK,' said Snowden finally. 'I'm here to support you, no matter what.' He smiled. 'Even if it DOES mean breaking every single rule and putting ourselves in grave danger.'

'That's more like it!' cheered Droplett. She jumped up and down a little too enthusiastically and caused a downpour of rain all over Ray's bed. 'Oops. I don't suppose there's any rainbow weather magic that dries stuff?'

And the friends burst out laughing.

'We'll need to blend in as much as possible when

we're ON Earth,' said Ray, stuffing everything into her bag, including snacks, sky juice, and an atlas full of Earth maps. 'And I'll bring the Britolian Museum book with the picture of the rainbow staff. I found the museum address at the back of the book, so I've marked it on the map with a smiley face. I *think* that's everything.'

'How about my rain cape?' asked Droplett. 'Should I take it off?'

'Probably best,' said Ray. 'And Snowden, you might need to tone down on the snowy clothing.'

Snowden sighed as he slipped off his snow gloves. 'This feels SO weird,' he said, placing them neatly into his satchel.

Droplett gasped. 'It looks weird. I don't think I've ever seen your actual hands before.'

'Well,' said Snowden. 'They look like hands really.' He wiggled his fingers around, and an eruption of snowflakes poured from his palm. He yelped and wafted them away. 'Aargh! I don't have NEARLY as much control without my snow gloves!'

'And THAT is why our unique weather

instruments are so important!' said Ray with a side smile.

'OK, OK,' said Snowden, nudging his friend lightly. 'I said I'd go, didn't I?'

'Keep your cape and gloves with you though, JUST in case of weather magic emergencies,' said Ray.

'Do you think Nim will be OK carrying the three of us ALL the way to Earth?' asked Snowden.

Ray looked up at the cloud-cat busy washing himself with one eye on his bottom. 'I'm sure it'll be fine,' she said, not entirely convinced by her own words.

She grabbed the spotty shower cap her dad had brought home for her and pulled it over her rainbow hair as a disguise. Then she stuck two

second-class stamps on her cheek.
Now she felt like a REAL explorer!

Suddenly, her bedroom door swung open.
Ray swiftly kicked her fully packed bag under her
bed out of sight.

'Hi, Mum!' she said brightly.

'WE'RE NOT PLANNING AN ADVENTURE
AT ALL,' shouted Droplett.

'Well, I'd hope not,' Cloudia said. 'That would
be a VERY silly idea. But, Ray, good news! I'm
going to see the head of the Council of
Forecasters right now, so stay here – I won't be
long . . .'

Ray waited to hear her mum leave in a cloud-
cab before grabbing her bag and turning to her
friends. 'Right. Let's go to EARTH!'

'Um . . . I'm not sure that's going to be
possible after all,' said Snowden, peering out
of the window.

Ray hadn't anticipated that the hordes of
reporters would be back, surrounding Cloud
Nine. 'Wobbling weathervanes!' She furrowed

her eyebrows, then looked at Nim, who'd
re-formed since his explosion with two heads.
'I have an idea!' she said.

The friends huddled together and kept as quiet as
possible. They were tucked *inside* Nim's floofy
body as the cloud-cat casually glided across the
sky in the shape of a rather suave unicorn.

'Who does this stray cloud-creature belong
to?' Ray heard a reporter call out.

Ray held her breath and squeezed Snowden's
and Droplett's hands.

'It's probably Marie La Waft's. She's ALWAYS
losing her cloud-unicorn!' Ray heard another
reporter reply.

Nim sped up a little. Slowly but surely, the
reporter's voice faded away. Ray peeked out from
Nim's cloud body and was relieved to see the
Weatherlands already behind them.

'The coast is clear, guys!' she said.

The three friends zipped across the skies on

the back of Nim, praying he wouldn't explode.

'Look at all the treeeeeees!' sang Droplett, bouncing up and down as the land below came into view. 'Oooh, and that big bird flying towards us!'

'That's not a bird,' said Snowden, sitting up a little straighter, his eyes growing to the size of plates. 'That's an aeroplane!'

He grabbed Nim by the ears and swerved him out of the way JUST in time to avoid being hit by the huge jet flying past them.

Ray spotted all the humans at the windows. 'What if they see us?' she said, covering her face with her arms.

'Don't worry, humans can only see Weatherlings when we touch the ground,' said Snowden.

'Well, thank the skies for that,' breathed Ray.

The gang kept on flying until they approached a huge city. Tall buildings of all different shapes decorated the skyline, and countless humans looked like tiny bugs scurrying across the network of streets. Ray pulled her compass out from her pocket and checked it against the atlas map to make sure they were heading the right way.

Thankful not to bump into any Forecasters or Weather Warriors on the way, Ray and the gang finally reached their destination; a grand-looking building supported by large columns. Enormous steps led to the main door. Nim hovered a few metres above the ground in a quiet corner of the museum square.

'Nim, I need you to hide under my hat, OK?' said Ray, pulling up the shower cap.

The friends stepped on to solid ground, and the cloud-cat shrank to the size of a pea, before nestling on Ray's head underneath the puffy bonnet.

'You ready?' Ray asked her friends. 'We need to act as human-y as possible.'

As the gang entered the museum, Ray

almost stumbled backwards with surprise. It was *much* bigger on the inside than it looked on the outside. Rooms led to more rooms, which led to stairs and other rooms. Old pots and carvings and tapestries lined the walls behind shiny glass cases, as well as ancient jewellery, clothing and books.

'I want to live here!' Ray breathed. 'Just look at all these treasures! La Blaze found a pretty pot JUST like that one!' she said, pointing to a strangely shaped vessel inside one of the cabinets. 'I bet La Blaze would LOVE this place. I read in one of her books that she was planning on opening up a Museum of Earthly Curiosities in Celestia!'

Snowden's ears began spurting with snowflakes. 'Look at all the old books!' he said in awe.

Droplett placed her hands over his ears. 'You need to STOP with your snow-plosions if you want to stay here for more than five minutes!' she hissed.

'Where do we even start? There's SO MUCH to look at,' said Ray, feeling a little overwhelmed.

They began to wander through room after room filled with ancient artefacts, trying their very best not to get too distracted.

'There's more than one floor,' said Snowden, pointing towards a map on the wall.

'I guess we work our way up?' Ray suggested.

They entered a room full of larger glass cases. Inside the cases were painted coffins, skulls and bones, amongst other strange objects.

'Why is that person sleeping in there?!' asked Droplett, pointing at a withered body wrapped in dirty rags inside one of the enclosures. She knocked on the glass. 'Hellooooo? Wakey-wakey!' She frowned and read the small sign next to the body. 'EEE-JIP-SHUN-MUMMY . . . Wait, WHAT? That's someone's mum?!' A few adults on the other side of the glass gave Droplett a disapproving glance.

Snowden guided her away gently. 'Mummies

aren't the same thing as mums . . .and well, they're not exactly sleeping,' he whispered.

'Well, if they're not sleeping, then what are–' Droplett's eyes grew wide. 'OH!' Then she grimaced. 'EWW!'

Ray led the way through the room of mummys then up a spiral staircase to a collection animal skeletons. 'WHY IS EVERYTHING IN THIS PLACE SO DEAD?' cried Droplett.

For the next hour, the friends climbed up what felt like a BAZILLION stairs, rushing through room after room and checking every object, but the rainbow staff was nowhere to be seen. They searched a hall of old paintings (Droplett was VERY impressed with the moustaches) and an exhibit of rather scary statues (Snowden did NOT like those).

FINALLY the friends reached the very top floor
of the museum. Above two big wooden doors a
sign read: *The Oldest Treasures in the World*. Ray
took a deep breath as she walked past glass cases
filled with trinkets, plaques, coins and other
beautiful treasures.

'Maybe the staff isn't here any more,' Ray
muttered to herself. If her rainbow
instrument wasn't here, then she
had NO IDEA where it could be.
But then something glimmered
in the corner of her eye and
she ran over to a tall, narrow
glass cabinet at the very end
of the room. There it was.

The long golden staff
shone under the museum
lights. Two rings at the top
with two golden wings.
It was beautiful.

'It's SO SHINY!' said
Droplett, squashing her nose

up against the glass.

Ray waited for a small group of schoolchildren to leave the room, before running to the large wooden doors at the entrance and heaving them shut. Then she turned to her friends.

'Snowden, you're going to need to put your snow gloves on,' she said firmly.

'What are you up to?' said Snowden warily.

'We're going to get that rainbow staff,' Ray said with determination. 'But I need you to use a snow spell to freeze the door handles to stop anyone coming in while we get it.'

Snowden slipped on his embroidered gloves and got to work, drawing a beautiful snowflake in the air. The snowflake twisted and turned before slithering around the door handles and forming a block of ice.

'Good job!' said Ray.

'How are we going to get the staff out of the cabinet without smashing through the glass?' asked Droplett.

'We need someone small enough to fit into

that cabinet,' said Ray. 'And someone who can get inside without breaking in . . .'

Droplett's eyes lit up.

'Do you think you could puddle-port inside and retrieve the staff?' asked Ray hopefully.

'Easy breezy!' said Droplett with a salute. 'I shall do my VERY BEST puddle-porting!'

Droplett pulled on her rain cape, which she'd had tucked into her trousers. With one big swish, she disappeared into her own puddle. Seconds later she reappeared, pressed up behind the glass in the cabinet, shimmying her way along the tiny space. With a thumbs up she carefully lifted the staff and tucked it under her arm. With another swish she was gone, reappearing between Ray and Snowden.

As soon as Ray gripped the long metal handle, she felt something shift inside her. Her fingers tingled. Colours filled her vision – red, orange, yellow, green, blue, indigo and violet. They swirled and twisted and flowed through her mind, through her veins, through her body and out through the staff. 'This is definitely MY weather instrument!' she cried.

The handles on the large wooden doors began to jiggle.

'Hey, it won't open!' said a voice.

'Let me try,' said another. Another jiggle.

'How are we meant to get out of here without somebody thinking we've stolen the staff?' said Snowden.

BANG BANG BANG

There was no way out . . . But Ray couldn't possibly leave without the rainbow staff now she'd finally found it.

CHAPTER 16

PUDDLE-PORT

'There *might* be a way,' said Droplett.

Ray gripped the staff. 'Droplett. You're not suggesting we –'

'Puddle-port!' sang Droplett, bracing her rain cape.

'Have you ever tried puddle-porting WITH another Weatherling?' asked Ray.

'Well, it worked with the staff and the rumblebuns at the festival,' said Droplett with a shrug. 'So why not?'

'How about, because we're actual living creatures!' squeaked Snowden.

Ray grabbed Droplett's hand. 'I trust you, Droplett,' she said bravely.

Snowden sighed. 'I don't really have a choice, do I?' he said.

'OK,' said Droplett. 'When we're puddle-porting, keep your eyes closed, your mouth shut, do NOT let go of my hand and do not, under ANY circumstances, fart.'

'What happens if we let go?' asked Snowden.

'You'll probably be floating around in the puddle on Earth forever.'

Snowden's face went a little pale.

'Ready?' asked Droplett.

Ray nodded.

'Nope,' said Snowden, closing his eyes tight.

Droplett swished her rain cape JUST as the museum doors burst open – and Ray found herself being pulled into a huge puddle as if she were made of rainwater itself. Water rushed past her ears. She was quite sure her stomach had been left somewhere in the museum. It was hard not to scream. But she remembered what Droplett said and pressed her lips together tightly. She could feel Droplett's hand still gripping hers tightly, and within a few seconds, Ray felt solid ground beneath her.

When she opened her eyes, she was standing in a puddle outside the museum.

Snowden was a little wobbly on his feet and a rather unpleasant shade of green. His cheeks puffed out and he vomited straight back into the puddle.

'You opened your mouth, didn't you?' said Droplett. She swished her cape, making the puddle disappear. 'Let's hope I never open *that* puddle portal again.'

Nim popped out of Ray's shower cap with a POOF and expanded so that the friends could climb on to his back. A real-life cat feeding on some scraps from a bin hissed at them.

'I didn't think anyone could see us unless we touched Earth?' asked Droplett.

'That's what I thought,' said Ray. 'But I've heard real cats see EVERYTHING.'

The journey back to the Weatherlands was smooth, and Ray used the 'hiding inside Nim's unicorn cloud-form' trick to get back to Cloud

Nine. The friends landed in Ray's bedroom, climbed out of Nim's cloudy belly and headed to the kitchen as casually as possible to fetch some lunch.

Ray stopped at the bottom of the stairs and gasped. Snowden started sneezing snowballs. Because sitting at the kitchen table with her mum . . . were none other than La Blaze DeLight and Coo La La.

'Ray Grey, you are in *deep* trouble,' said Cloudia calmly. 'And the only reason I am not shouting is because we have *guests*.' She smiled WAY too sweetly. 'So, would you care to tell me WHERE YOU HAVE BEEN?'

'Well, I, we, uh . . .' stammered Ray, her tongue twisting in knots. She couldn't believe La Blaze was inside her house – but Ray also couldn't believe she was in trouble in front of her either.

La Blaze was pretending not to listen while taking sips of Ozonian tea. Coo La La made it clear he WAS listening, eating from a tiny tub of popcorn and watching Cloudia and Ray in turn.

CHAPTER 17

KNOWLEDGE IS POWER

'WELL?' Cloudia snapped.

Ray sighed before telling her mum the truth.

'It was all my idea,' said Ray. 'I suggested we go to Earth to find my rainbow instrument.'

She held up the shiny, winged staff. Both Cloudia and La Blaze gasped.

'You went to Earth AGAIN . . . ?' shrieked Cloudia.

La Blaze gazed at the staff, her eyes wide.

'I found out that my weather instrument was in the Britolean Museum! I know I shouldn't have gone, but I NEED the instrument to control my new power!' Ray pleaded. She bowed her head. 'I'm really sorry.'

Cloudia was silent. Ray knew that her mother was another level of angry when she didn't say anything at all. She had no doubt she'd be grounded for AT LEAST a year.

La Blaze gently placed a hand on Cloudia's shoulder. 'Mrs Grey, how about you go have a nice sit-down? I'll have a little chat to Ray.'

Cloudia frowned. 'Well,' she finally said. 'If Ray isn't going to listen to me, maybe she'll listen to you . . .'

She took her teacup and left the kitchen, not before giving her daughter one last disappointed glance. Ray felt terrible for making her mum feel so worried. And now she was about to get told off by La Blaze. This was quite possibly the WORST day ever.

'Why don't we all sit down,' said La Blaze, gesturing to the empty chairs around the kitchen table. 'There's a lot to discuss.'

Snowden's nose was positively streaming with tiny snowballs. His eyes were watery and his cheeks puffy.

Coo La La gazed at him in repulsion. 'What is wrong with YOU, child?'

'ACHOOOOO!' Snowden spluttered. 'I think I might be allergic to you,' he said.

La Blaze closed the kitchen door, and joined the friends at the table.

Here we go, thought Ray. Time to get a telling-off by her absolute hero.

But to Ray's surprise, La Blaze grinned then whispered, 'This is so exciting!' She leaned in closer. 'I saw the newspapers, Ray! Then I remembered meeting you at the Eclipse Festival, and thought, I MUST come and find out exactly what happened! You found a magical treasure?'

Ray couldn't believe it. La Blaze remembered her. And now she was totally on Ray's side. Today had suddenly turned from the worst to the BEST day ever!

'I felt like a REAL Earth Explorer, JUST like YOU!' Ray said with a grin. 'I found the treasure which was marked in the rainbow book you signed for me. It was a black crystal with rainbow weather magic INSIDE it! Then somehow, during the Eclipse, the magic burst out of the crystal and went into ME!' She proudly held up a lock of bright blue hair.

'Ray can control other Weatherlings' magic!' Droplett added.

'And the winged staff we found in the museum matched the symbol on the big Rainbow Weatherstone!' said Snowden as a stream of think-flakes slowly wafted around a disgusted Coo La La's head.

'There's a Rainbow Weatherstone?' said La Blaze.

'Yes!' said Ray. 'It BURST right out from the ground!'

'And this all happened *during* the Eclipse?'

Ray nodded.

'Ray, this is extraordinary,' said La Blaze. 'You have PROVED rainbow weather magic is real! As an Earth Explorer, this is the perfect subject matter for my next book!'

Ray almost fell off of her chair. 'BOOK?' she gasped.

'I want to write ALL about your big adventure, Ray and find out about this rainbow weather magic!' said La Blaze.

'Wobbling weathervanes,' said Ray, blushing, unable to comprehend what La Blaze was saying. 'I don't know much about this magic yet. There's no information about it anywhere . . . So, I'm not REALLY sure what I'm doing!'

'Well, that's the super exciting part!' said La Blaze, her eyes wide with excitement. 'I can help you, Ray! Exploring isn't just about finding treasure – it's about discovering NEW things. And this is quite possibly the BEST discovery ever!' La Blaze didn't seem to blink once. 'Do you still have the black crystal?'

Ray shook her head. 'It disappeared.'

'Intriguing!' La Blaze scratched her head in deep thought.

'But we think a Rogue might have buried it, perhaps to hide the trapped rainbow weather magic,' said Snowden.

'Hmmm, that does seem plausible,' La Blaze

agreed. 'We must investigate *more* about this crystal – try to find out WHERE it came from, HOW it was made . . .' The Sun Weatherling looked very serious all of a sudden. 'Being a Rainbow Weatherling means you are capable of BIG things, Ray,' she said. 'YOU are now incredibly valuable to the Weatherlands. HOWEVER . . .' She paused, and her eyes grew dark. 'As valuable as you are to the Weatherlands and the world, you are an even bigger THREAT to the Rogues.'

Ray felt the hairs on the back of her neck prickle.

'We must act fast,' continued La Blaze. 'The Rogues will surely know of the return of the rainbow weather magic. You threaten ALL of their plans, Ray. They'll be doing *everything* they possibly can to stop you. If we find out how that black crystal trapped the rainbow weather magic, then maybe – just *maybe* – we can use it to trap the Rogues' magic!'

'Oh! That's a great idea!' said Ray,

clapping her hands together.

La Blaze stood up. 'Just think, Ray. If YOU harnessed such a crystal, you'd be unstoppable. Take control of a Rogue's magic, then BAM! Trap their magic for good!'

Ray digested this. 'There'd never be a storm on Earth ever again,' she said to herself.

La Blaze lowered her sunglasses. 'Exactly,' she said. 'But we must find out what this black crystal is. That is our goal. Knowledge is power, after all.'

The door opened and Ray's mother appeared holding her Compass Caller. She still looked angry. 'Ray,' she said. 'The head of the Council of Forecasters has arranged to see you tomorrow.'

Ray gulped. 'OK Mum,' she said quietly.

'You have nothing to worry about, kid,' said La Blaze reassuringly. 'It's not like you're conspiring with a Rogue. You have brand-new powers that haven't been seen for over a thousand years, and they'll just want to ask you a few questions.'

Ray strained a smile. 'I guess,' she said.

CHAPTER 18

BEARD!

LA BLAZE
FINDS BIGGEST
PUMPKIN

After La Blaze's visit, Ray was sent to her room and Snowden and Droplett were sent home. Ray wished she didn't have to wait until tomorrow for her big meeting with the Council of Forecasters. But Ray was also super excited to have La Blaze on her side!

She sat on her bed for the rest of the evening looking through her *La Blaze Annual of DeLights*, with Nim nuzzled in her lap. At dinner time, Cloudia hardly spoke. Ray felt terrible for worrying her mum so much. She really hoped her dad would return home soon. Once the family were back together, they'd be able to talk about everything over a platter of pitter-patter pancakes and perhaps everything would feel normal again.

Ray woke up to the sound of Nim exploding, and she could have sworn she'd heard the flapping of wings. She was lying face down on her La Blaze annual, a puddle of dribble pooling from her mouth. Ray groaned and pulled herself up and rubbed her eyes. It was the next morning already!

When she got downstairs, it was very quiet. Her mum must still be in bed, which was unusual. Maybe she was exhausted from being so worried, thought Ray with a heavy heart. Whilst Nim gobbled down his bowl of frost-bites, bowl and all, Ray took the opportunity to make her mum a big breakfast to say sorry.

She sprinkled eggshells into the shape of a heart, and inside, the letters S O R I, then knocked lightly on her parents' bedroom door ready to present her apology breakfast.

'Mum? Are you awake? I made you something.' Ray opened the door a little. She was surprised to see the bed fully made. 'Mum?' she called out. 'Are you already up?'

Maybe she had gone to get some more silver

lining, Ray thought. The whole house was wobbling precariously, hanging on by one silvery thread. But another hour passed, and Ray's mum still wasn't home.

Ray hugged her rainbow staff to her chest as she sat on her bed wondering what to do. Then she spotted something she hadn't noticed before.

There was a teeny-weeny engraving along the rim of the top ring. It could only be seen if you angled the staff just right in the sunlight. On closer inspection, Ray noticed five little symbols. They looked like snowflakes.

She decided to call her friends on the Compass Caller. If anyone knew snowflakes, it was Snowden!

'That looks like ancient snow runes,' Snowden said, munching on a drizzle-pickle sandwich.

The friends had arrived in no time and were sitting on Ray's bed studying the strange snowflake symbols engraved on the staff.

'What do they mean?!' asked Droplett,

jumping up and down and soaking Snowden's
sandwich before he'd had a chance to finish it,
as usual.

'Do you know any ancient snow weather magic,
Snowden?' Ray asked hopefully.

Snowden pushed his glasses a little further up
his nose. 'Granny Everfreeze has taught me the odd
rune or two. It's quite complicated.' He tugged at
his snow gloves. 'I can give it a try, though.'

He gobbled down the rest of
his soggy sandwich and studied
the snow symbols on the staff.
'I think I've got it,' he said with
a nod. He began to draw the
snowflake runes in the air.
'Ancient snow weather magic
works a little differently,' he said,
not taking his eyes off the floating
flakes. 'One has to repeat the snow
runes again, but backwards, adding
accents to every other third arm of
the snowflake ...'

Droplett blew a raspberry. 'You sound like you're speaking in riddles.'

Once Snowden had finished the intricate dots and dashes and lines and swirls, the snowflakes hung in mid-air for a moment before swirling and morphing into a single word.

BEARD

'Beard?' Ray repeated.

She felt her hands tingle and the rainbow staff began to glow!

'Wobbling weathervanes!' Ray gasped, holding the staff at arm's length. A very thin stream of colours stretched away from the tip of the staff and out of Ray's bedroom window.

'Well, that's weird,' said Droplett.

'It looks like it's leading somewhere,' said Ray, straining her eyes to see where the thin line of colours was heading.

'No sneaking out, Ray,' warned Snowden. 'Don't you think you're in enough trouble?'

'Mum and Dad aren't home,' said Ray. 'We'll just have a look to see where the colours are leading.

It might tell us some more about my magic.'

Snowden sighed, and Droplett grinned.
'Let's follow that rainbow!' she said.

The friends climbed on Nim's back and
followed the colours across the sky. They
stretched over the Cloudimulus Suburbs, over
the Crackling Caves and all the way through the
Valley of Winds, until they disappeared into
the treetops of the Forest of Farenheits.

'It's leading to the Weatherstone Circle!'
said Ray.

Sure enough, the colours stopped at the large
Rainbow Weatherstone in the centre of the circle.
The Weatherstone was also glowing brightly. As
Ray approached, the face of the Weatherstone
began to shift, revealing a large rainbow-coloured
hole.

'WHAT THE DRIP-DROP?' yelped Droplett.

'Sizzling snowflakes!' cried Ray. She stepped
back a little, and the hole shrank. She stepped
forward. The hole grew again.

'It's getting bigger as you get nearer to it,

Ray,' said Snowden. He slowly moved his gloved hand towards the shimmering rainbow void.

'Snowden . . . be careful!' urged Ray, worried for her friend.

To her relief, his hand simply glided through the face of the stone, as if it wasn't there at all.

'It seems like a magical doorway?' said Ray. 'Maybe the word BEARD was some kind of secret password . . .'

The void suddenly disappeared with a POP.

'Oh! I think you just closed it again,' said Droplett.

Ray repeated the word 'BEARD' as loudly as she could, and the rainbow doorway swirled into view once again.

Ray placed one foot inside the whirling entrance. Snowden gulped. Droplett's eyes were wild with excitement.

'Are you coming then?' said Ray, walking right through the colours.

Suddenly the solid ground gave way beneath her. She was sliding at top speed along a rainbow, screaming at the top of her voice . . . but as she sped along the colourful ribbons, she decided that this was actually rather FUN. It was hard not to have fun on a slide.

Ray held her staff up as she descended further and further, with Nim close behind.

'GAAAAAAAAAAAAAAAAAAAAAAH!' Snowden shot past her at an alarming speed, followed by Droplett bringing up the rear and screaming, 'I DON'T EVEN CARE IF WE'RE ABOUT TO DIE – WE'RE DOING IT IN STYLE!'

Ray was surprised when they started to slow down, skidding neatly to a halt at the bottom.

'THAT WAS AMAZING!' said Droplett, bouncing up and down on the spot. 'AGAIN!'

But Ray stood quietly. 'Wow!' she gasped, taking in her surroundings.

They were standing in a large underground burrow. Sunflower lanterns sprang to life around them and snow gently fell from the ceiling. Tiny cloud-creatures skipped around the walls, and rumbles of thunder created a low musical hum.

'This place is alive with weather magic!'
said Ray.

The walls were intertwined with tree roots that
fizzled with tiny zip-zaps of lightning, and a light
breeze jingled a pretty wind chime dangling from
the centre of the burrow. Covering one side of the
wall were hundreds of drawings and notes tucked
into the roots, and half a cup of ozonian tea was
still perched on large wooden desk as if the whole
place had been frozen in time.

'It's like a secret base!' said Droplett,
wriggling with excitement.

Ray walked over to the desk, covered in books
and paper. Amongst the mess lay a large notebook
with shiny writing on its cover. It said:

PROPERTY OF
PROFESSOR RAINBOW BEARD.

CHAPTER 19
FAMILY REUNION

'Is rainbow beard some kind of hairstyle?' asked Droplett curiously.

Snowden cleared his throat and pointed to a large picture on the wall. 'I think you'll find that Rainbow Beard is a name . . . And it looks like he was one of the ancient Rainbow Weatherlings that disappeared all those years ago!'

Ray and Droplett rushed over to Snowden's side and gazed at the picture. There were small illustrations of a whole group of Weatherlings. Each of them had rainbow-coloured hair, and had coloured eyes that didn't match, just like Ray's!

Amongst the pictures were the words RAINBOW SCHOOL PROFESSORS.

'There was a Rainbow School?!' gasped Droplett.

'I could do with one of those right now!' said Ray. 'It looks like Rainbow Beard was the head teacher!' She gestured to the very top picture of a wise-looking man with a VERY long beard, and the name PROFESSOR RAINBOW BEARD written below.

Droplett began to read out the names scribbled beneath some of the teachers. 'Rainbow Twist, Rainbow Rewind, Rainbow Slide . . .'

PROFESSOR RAINBOW BEARD

RAINBOW SCHOOL PROFESSORS

RAINBOW REWIND

RAINBOW SLIDE

RAINBOW TWIST

RAINBOW VANISH

RAINBOW BRAID

'I wonder why they had such odd names?' chuckled Ray.

Snowden, who had been exploring the burrow like a cloud-cat searching for treats, picked up a book from Rainbow Beard's desk and gasped, his ears spurting with a long stream of think-flakes. '*The Magic of Rainbows*!' he read aloud, pointing to the cover. 'Ray, this is the same book you found in the library! Well, a version that isn't as tatty and completely torn to shreds.'

Ray recognised the picture of a large rainbow stretching across the cover with the colourful-haired lady beneath, holding a large staff just like Ray's.

'Does it have the map with the cross inside?' asked Ray.

Snowden flicked through the pages to where the map was and, sure enough, a big fat cross was scribbled on it. Next to it said: THE OLDEST TREE IN THE WORLD, LOCATION OF SUNFLOWER ECLIPSE PARTY.

'Oh,' said Ray feeling a little surprised. 'So the X marks the spot wasn't marking a buried treasure at all. It was marking the location of a party?!'

Snowden flicked to a chapter titled RAINBOW LORE. 'Maybe this will tell you more about how your magic works . . .'

He read aloud: 'Every Rainbow Weatherling has the power to control another Weatherling's magic . . .'

'Well, we certainly know you can do THAT, Ray!' Droplett interrupted with a wink.

Snowden continued, 'But as well as the power to control another, every Rainbow Weatherling is also born with one additional rainbow gift, whether it be making rainbow slides, creating rainbow forcefields, or twisting one weather magic into another. No two Rainbow Weatherlings have the same unique gift . . .'

Snowden's ear erupted with an explosion of snowflakes.

'That's why they have funny names!' the friends gasped in unison.

'Each name must relate to their special

rainbow gift!' Ray smiled. That was a nice thought.

'I'm very intrigued about Rainbow BEARD's gift!' Snowden added with a smirk.

Droplett turned to Ray. 'Hey, I wonder what unique gift YOU have?' she asked. 'I REALLY hope it's making rainbow slides!'

Ray pondered, then her eyes grew wide. 'Wait. If all the Rainbow Weatherlings' magic was trapped in that black crystal I found and ALL of that magic then went into ME during the Eclipse, then that means . . .'

'YOU must have ALL the rainbow gifts!' Droplett blurted out, exploding with a shower of raindrops. 'You're like a SUPER DUPER version of a Rainbow Weatherling!'

Ray gulped as her friends grinned at her. It was slowly becoming clear just how much power she actually possessed.

'If you've got ALL the gifts, then what would your rainbow name be?' asked Droplett, dancing from one foot to the other.

'If Ray named herself after every gift then that's

going to be a very long name . . .' said Snowden. 'Plus we don't even know how many gifts you have floating around inside you – there could be hundreds!'

Ray suddenly felt a little woozy. 'This is a LOT to take on board,' she said breathlessly and closed her eyes for a moment.

'I've been Ray Grey all my life. It would be strange to suddenly change my whole name,' she finally said to her friends. 'I can't imagine being anyone else really.'

'Then don't be.' Snowden smiled. 'Just be you.'

'Be me,' Ray muttered. Then a smile slowly spread across her face. 'OK then. How about . . . Rainbow Grey?'

'Rainbow Grey . . .' Droplett and Snowden repeated at the same time.

'And you can still be called Ray for short,' said Droplett with a wink. 'It's PERFECT!'

'Exactly!' Ray stood up tall, bracing her rainbow staff, and yelled out, 'BEHOLD RAINBOW GREY!' before spinning around happily on the spot and falling over with dizziness.

'I think we should try out some of your rainbow gifts!' cheered Droplett, rummaging through all the weather spells stuck in the roots around the walls. 'Oooh, YES! Let's try this one!' She pointed to a picture of Rainbow Slide gliding across a ribbon of colours bursting from her staff.

'I guess I could give it a go,' said Ray with a nervous laugh. 'To see if I really do have all these rainbow gifts inside me!'

'Right, I'll read out the instructions . . .' said Droplett, clearing her throat.

Ray stood, staff in hand, ready for action.

'OK,' said Droplett. 'Hold your staff directly in front of you in a vertical position.' Ray did as she was told. 'Next, swing it over your head, and back again as if painting a large brushstroke in the air, and then JUMP.'

Ray nodded firmly. She lifted up her staff, moving it along an invisible curve backwards over her head, then forward. She felt her rainbow weather magic flood through her body, her arms,

her fingers,
through the
staff and
WHOOOOOOOOSH –
colours extended through the air.
'It's working!' she cheered.

Ray took a deep breath, bent her knees,
then pushed herself off the ground.

Almost effortlessly, she found herself flying
through the air, following the arc of the rainbow
she'd created. But Ray had misjudged the height
of the burrow and managed to wedge herself
between the top of the rainbow and the ceiling.

'Think I might need some more practice!' she
said with a strained smile.

The rainbow slide began to fade, and Ray went
tumbling to the floor with a BOMP. Another
bruise to add to the collection on her bottom,
no doubt.

Snowden suddenly sneezed,
sending a small army of snowballs
scattering across the room.

'EWWW!' cried Droplett,
trying to avoid the snow-snot.
'You had better not have a cold!'

'Or a hot,' Ray added.

'No, no,' sniffed Snowden.
'I don't FEEL ill. I think my allergies are
flaring up again.' He rubbed his red nose.
'AAAACHOO!'

As Ray narrowly avoided another mini
avalanche of snotty snowballs she spotted
something among the notes and drawings
scattered across the floor. An envelope.
It said:

*To a Future Rainbow
Weatherling*

CHAPTER 20
THE LETTER

Droplett and Snowden gathered round as Ray pulled out a neatly written letter.

Dear Reader,
I was a teacher of rainbow weather magic. Our magic brought good to the world, taming a Rogue's wrath. Rainbow Weatherlings worked closely with the Woodlings, creating peace, balance and harmony between the Earth and skies.

'Woodlings?' muttered Ray. 'Who are they?'

Every eleven years the Rainbow Weatherlings and the Woodlings gathered at the Oldest Tree for a party to celebrate the Sunflower Eclipse. This eleven-year Eclipse was a special moment when Earth and sky would truly unite as one. But the peace and balance was shattered when one Rainbow Weatherling chose POWER over unity. Rainbow Twist, once a respected teacher of Rainbow Academy, discovered something so deadly, it would END peace between the Earth and skies. By destroying the trees on Earth, a malevolent darkness would be released. The very essence of the tree's sadness.

This Shadow Essence was the opposite to everything a rainbow represented. For as bright and hopeful as a rainbow was, the Shadow Essence was as dark and hopeless – an abyss.

Growing more powerful every day, Rainbow Twist formed an army of Rogues. She went by the name Tornadia, and with her army behind her, Tornadia orchestrated her own storm, known as Storm Tornadia.

On the night of the Eclipse, when she knew every Rainbow Weatherling would be gathered around the Oldest Tree, Tornadia and her Rogues destroyed the tree, releasing its Shadow Essence.

The older the tree, the more life it had to be destroyed, and the stronger the essence. The Rainbow Weatherlings could not fight this darkness. But neither could Tornadia. She underestimated the power of the Shadow Essence and she was never seen again. But though she was gone, her storm still raged on.

The only reason I am here, is because of my darling Cloud Weatherling wife who found me and flew me back to the Weatherlands. She helped me regain strength, but my magic was well and truly gone and my rainbow staff was lost to the storm on Earth.

We now have a beautiful baby girl, but she has been born with no weather magic. I live in hope that someone will find this letter, and that maybe, just maybe, rainbow weather magic will return to my family one day.

For every storm, a rainbow WILL follow.
Forever hoping,

Professor Rainbow Beard

'Wobbling weathervanes,' breathed Ray. 'Rainbow Beard must be my ancestor, if he was the only Rainbow Weatherling left in the Weatherlands . . . THIS explains why my family on Mum's side hasn't had any weather magic for so long! AND why the rainbow weather magic went into me . . . We were Rainbow Weatherlings all along and we didn't even know it!'

'It makes sense,' said Snowden. 'And that must be Rainbow Beard's staff!' He pointed to the long golden instrument.

'But why didn't some of the rainbow weather magic go back to your mum too, when it broke free from the shadow crystal?' asked Droplett.

'I guess I was the only one there at the time the crystal opened inside the stone circle,' said Ray. 'So I was the only one to receive all the magic.'

'Well, I can't quite believe that Tornadia Twist – responsible for the BIGGEST storm on Earth – was once a RAINBOW Weatherling too!' said Droplett.

'That's dark stuff,' said Snowden. 'In more

ways than one! Who'd have thought that the destruction of trees created the Shadow Essence?'

Ray felt as if a big sunflower had ignited in her head. 'This explains why I found the black crystal buried beneath the Oldest Tree in the World. When the Shadow Essence absorbed all the Rainbow Weatherlings' magic, it must have eventually crystallised into what I thought was treasure.'

'I think you're right, Ray!' said Snowden, looking impressed.

'We should tell La Blaze about everything we've discovered!' said Ray. 'She wanted to write all about how the black crystal was made – now we know! As she said, if we find out how that black crystal trapped the rainbow weather magic, then maybe we can use it to trap the ROGUES' magic and stop them once and for all!'

But Snowden shook his head. 'Rainbow Beard's letter said that the Shadow Essence only affected rainbow weather magic, nobody else's,' he reminded Ray. 'So I don't see how it can stop the Rogues. If we're going to tell anyone about this, we should tell the Council of Forecasters first.'

'I agree with snow-boy on this one,' said Droplett.

Ray frowned. 'But we can trust La Blaze! She's on my side!'

'I don't know, Ray,' said Droplett, shuffling awkwardly. 'This Shadow Essence sounds really scary. We don't want this information getting into the wrong hands, especially as the Rogues could use the Shadow Essence against you!'

'As La Blaze said, your magic is a big threat to the Rogues,' said Snowden. 'No doubt they'll already be planning ways to stop you.'

'But La Blaze wants to help me,' said Ray. 'She's going to help me discover how my magic works!'

'Ray . . . you have everything you need RIGHT here,' said Droplett, spreading her arms out. 'You don't need La Blaze any more!'

Ray narrowed her eyes. 'I'm starting to think you don't like La Blaze,' she said quietly.

'No, Ray, we really like La Blaze,' said Snowden gently. 'But all this stuff about the Shadow Essence is very serious. The Council of Forecasters have to know first. They're a lot more important than La Blaze.'

'Plus, we don't REALLY know her,' added Droplett.

'La Blaze IS important - she's a grown-up,'
said Ray, feeling cross with her friends. 'And I
do know her. I know everything about her. '

'Well, you don't really KNOW know her,' said
Droplett, folding her arms. 'You've read all her
books but you've only met her twice.'

'I thought we'd agreed to support each other,
no matter what?' Ray said coldly.

'We ARE supporting you!' shouted Droplett.
'THAT'S why we think this really BIG discovery
should go straight to the most important
Weatherlings in the sky!'

Ray's cheeks felt very hot and her head was

beginning to ache. 'Y'know what? I think you're both just jealous,' she said.

'Jealous?' Droplett spluttered.

'Yes!' yelled Ray. 'You're jealous of La Blaze. Just because she wants to help me and write a book ALL about my magic!'

'That's not true!' Droplett yelled back at her. 'As if we're jealous of La Blaze! She's not even a famous explorer, nobody buys her books but YOU!'

Ray's blood was boiling. 'How can you say that?!' she snapped. 'La Blaze believes in me . . . ' Ray felt the words pouring out of her mouth but she was feeling too angry to stop. 'She's a true friend, unlike YOU!'

Droplett stared at Ray, her eyes looking shiny.

'Wait,' said Ray. 'I –'

But without even a splosh, Droplett puddle-ported away.

CHAPTER 21

BREAKING WIND!

'I didn't mean to say that,' Ray said, looking at Snowden. 'I'm so sorry.'

'We're just worried about you, Ray,' Snowden replied quietly. He looked so sad. 'We don't want anything bad to happen to you.'

Ray sighed.

A shuffling sound in the burrow made the friends jump. Snowden sneezed again.

'Droplett? Is that you?' called Ray, hoping her friend had come back to make up.

But nobody answered.

'Weird . . . It's probably just Nim messing around,' said Ray.

Snowden's face was puffy and his nose red. 'I should probably go home,' he said, trying desperately to hold in another sneeze. 'I've not seen much of Granny Everfreeze recently.'

'OK. I might stay here for a little longer,' said Ray, feeling glum.

After Snowden had left, Nim started pawing at the wall and miaowing.

'Stop that, Nim,' said Ray irritably. 'There's nothing there . . .'

Nim floated over to Ray and curled up in her lap.

'I'm sorry for being grumpy,' Ray sighed, sinking to the ground and holding Rainbow Beard's letter to her chest.

She yawned and watched the mini cloud-sheep dancing around the ceiling. She was quite sure Nim had eaten half of them. Her eyelids started to droop. Among the warmth of the sunflower lanterns, the gentle rumbles of thunder and soft crackles of the tiny lightning zaps, Ray fell into a deep sleep.

Ray awoke with a start. How long had she been asleep? Her mum would be so worried!

Bracing her rainbow staff, Ray made her way out of the secret burrow and into the Weatherstone Circle. The warm air hit her face and a patch of Greeting Gilliwiggles opened up their petals and wiggled their stems to say hello.

For a brief moment, everything felt OK. Then she remembered the horrible things she had said to her friends and a deep feeling of sadness overwhelmed her.

As Ray flew home across the skies on the back of Nim, she noticed that her family home was still dangling from Cloud Nine by just one silvery thread. It was very weird her mum hadn't fixed it yet. Nim landed on the mini balcony and Ray jumped off.

'Muuuum!' she called out.

Nothing. The house was empty.

Ray decided to turn on the Fizzogram for some company, spinning the dial until she found a good signal.

'BREAKING WIND!' the weather reporter declared. 'WEATHER WARRIORS FROM ALL

OVER THE WEATHERLANDS HAVE BEEN CALLED OUT TO THE BIGGEST STORM EVER ON EARTH YET. AN ARMY OF ROGUES ARE DEVASTATING THE WORLD'S OLDEST FOREST!'

'Oh no!' cried Ray. 'Nim, that means Dad will be fighting too, I hope he's OK!' She tried to listen for more news, but Nim was sniffing at something on the floor and hissing loudly.

'Nim? What's up with you?' Ray said.

She bent down to see a black and white speckled feather and picked it up for a closer look. This was all getting a bit strange . . .

Ray held her rainbow staff tightly.

'Something's not right here, Nim,' she said. 'Time to find out what's going on.'

The floofy cloud-cat expanded. Ray hopped on to his back and took to the Weatherland skies once more.

Soaring over the Flurry Mountains, Ray kept a close eye for any signs of her mum. She swept around Dripping-Down Village, and explored the

Crackling Caves, before checking every shop in the City of Celestia.

Ray asked Slap and Streak at the Rising Bun Bakery, but they hadn't seen Cloudia. She checked The Raining Champion cape store, A Cold Spell snow-glove fitters, and Gales and Arpeggios wind instruments – still no sign of her mum. Ray finally checked the For Every Cloud silver lining suppliers, where her mum visited every day without fail, but according to Mr Float, he'd not seen her mum today.

Ray gulped hard and ran out of the shop where Nim was waiting. The world around her felt distant. Her ears started to ring.

'Ray?' said a voice from far away. 'RAY?'

La Blaze was standing in front of her.

'Ray? Are you all right?' said La Blaze, shaking

Ray's shoulders gently.

'I can't find my mum . . .' Ray could barely say the words out loud. 'She hasn't been at home ALL day, and the silver lining is all broken, and she NEVER lets it get down to one thread . . .' Ray was sobbing now. 'And I was really mean to my friends, and there's a big storm on Earth and my dad is out there fighting it!'

'Shhh, take a breath, kid,' said La Blaze, pulling Ray into a hug. 'Everything's going to be OK. Look at me.'

Ray blinked the tears from her eyes and looked up at La Blaze's kind face.

'Let's calm down,' said La Blaze. 'I'll help you look for your mum.'

Coo La La swooped down from the skies, landing on La Blaze's shoulder and looking rather flustered. He cleared his throat and adjusted his monocle.

'Grave news,' he said seriously. 'I was flying back from my daily toilet break on Earth, and I just saw a bunch of Rogues escorting a woman with messy grey hair FULL of weird tools into the world's oldest forest!'

'W-what?!' croaked Ray. 'That sounds like Mum! I have to save her!'

She hopped on to Nim's back, ready to take flight. But La Blaze placed a hand on her shoulder.

'Stop right there,' she said. 'You're in no fit state to fly. Plus – no offence to Nim – but he's far too unreliable. I'LL take you to find your mum.'

'You'll help me?' asked Ray, gazing up at La Blaze as a long line of snot dripped down from her nostril and attached itself to her chin.

'Ray, of course I will help you,' said La Blaze. 'After *all* you've done for me.'

Ray wondered what above Earth she'd done for La Blaze. She gave a watery smile. 'Thank you. You really are the best.'

'Come on, I've got a great sun spell I use for getting around!' said La Blaze.

She held up her arms, and closed her eyes. Ray hadn't seen a lot of sun magic in action, since only the five SunKeeper families possessed such power. The sunflowers on La Blaze's wrists began to glow brightly. Shining beams swirled and twisted, finally creating the most beautiful sun-dragon. Ray gasped in awe as La Blaze mounted the glowing sun-creature, with Coo La La casually perched on her shoulder, reading a tiny newspaper.

'I had no idea sun magic could do THAT!' Ray spluttered.

'Ah, that's because SunKeepers are only allowed to use their magic to make the big Sunflower in the sky glow,' said La Blaze. 'But I'm not a SunKeeper, am I!' She shrugged. 'What are you waiting for?' La Blaze said as Ray stood there open-mouthed. 'Hop on. Let's go find your mum!'

CHAPTER 22
KNICKER-NADO

As the sun-dragon left the Weatherlands, Ray held on tight to La Blaze's waist, with Nim snuggled in her lap safely.

'Thank you,' she said quietly.

'Hmm?' said La Blaze, turning her head.

'Thank you for helping me,' said Ray. 'I don't know what I'd have done without you. And well – I know everything's going to be OK, because I'm with you.'

La Blaze kept her eyes front and guided the sun-dragon towards Earth. 'Well, kid, I'm sure you would've worked it out,' she said. 'You're a Rainbow Weatherling after all.'

Ray couldn't help noticing a sharp edge in La Blaze's voice. But there was no time to dwell on that, for the scene that had materialised below made Ray feel sick.

A HUGE forest criss-crossed by thousands of rivers and tiny towns was being ripped to shreds by Rogues of all sorts. A trickle of sweat ran down Ray's back, but she was unsure if this was due to the humid air or fear.

At least one hundred varieties of tornado whirled their way through the trees, as well as flocks of evil cloud-creatures – grey, murky and hulking as if made of ash, with deep red eyes, hungry for anything they could get their dirty paws on. Nim hissed at them and nuzzled further into Ray's belly for protection. Hailstones the size of geese rained down on the scene, as well as actual geese. A huge torrent of water narrowly missed Ray and La Blaze.

A thunder 'n' lightning pair of Rogues boshed their way through a pack of cloud-wolves, skiing on lightning bolts and shaking the fibres of the sky with mighty booms of thunder.

'EY BOSS!' one of them cried out with a jolly wave. Ray recognised their voices. It was the rogues called BOP and BLAP she'd seen when she went hunting for the treasure.

'BOSS! IT'S US! WHAT'S UP?!' they shouted again, looking in Ray's direction.

Who were they talking to? But there was no time for thinking as the sun-dragon nose-dived and Ray tumbled off its back through the sky.

'AAAAARGH!' she cried out, reaching for Nim, who was speeding along beside her.

She was swept sideways and then around and around. A pair of spotty knickers slapped her in the face. Uh oh. Squinting through the colours and patterns, Ray realised she was very much caught up in a large knicker-nado.

Ray held on to her rainbow staff tightly, still twisting and turning and now wearing at least fifteen pairs of knickers. She closed her eyes tight and tried to harness the same feelings as when she'd taken control of Frazzle's magic, and all the reporters' magic too . . . Every time, she'd felt a sense of urgency. And right now, she definitely felt that same feeling.

She opened her eyes and was relieved to see

a Rainbow pouring from her staff. Ray tried to maintain her focus. The colours wrapped themselves around and around the whirlwind of underwear, gradually tightening their grip. Ray suddenly felt a rush of wind blast through her insides as she finally took full control of the Wind Rogue's weather magic.

'Got ya!' whispered Ray.

'OI!' she heard from somewhere down below. 'GERROFF ME KNICKER COLLECTION!'

Ray swung her staff to one side. The knickers followed. She moved it to the other side and the windy knickers trailed along with her movements. She successfully transformed the once terrifying knicker-nado into an elegant display of garments, revealing the disgruntled Wind Rogue below. A tangled mop of messy grey fringe hung over her angry face, and she was wearing a baggy pair of stripy pantaloons and a large cape made purely from knickers. 'GIVE ME MY MAGIC BACK!' she screamed at

Ray, who was using the wind magic to stay afloat.

With the wind magic firmly in her grasp, Ray sent every single pair of knickers hurtling back towards the angry Rogue below. Ray watched as the spots and stripes and frills and sparkles chased the bewildered Wind Rogue away into the forest and out of sight, before she gently lowered herself to the ground, using the remains of the wind magic. Ray felt the power leave her as the Rogue ran further away in the trees.

For the first time ever, she'd actually felt in control of her power!

She was in the middle of the dense forest now, with the weather war still raging above and around her.

The air was humid, and full of chirrups and howls of hidden creatures. Ray found herself surrounded by a whole array of weird-looking plants she'd never seen before in the Weatherlands.

'Niiiiim!' Ray called out, suddenly panicking. 'Nim! Where are youuu?!'

Nim appeared with a POOF and a pair of stripy knickers on his head.

'Thank the skies,' said Ray, pulling the fluffy cloud-cat into her embrace. 'What happened to La Blaze?'

Ray was suddenly knocked sideways. She slid across the damp forest floor into a tree.

'YOU!' said an angry voice. 'DON'T FINK YOU CAN USE MY POWER AND GET AWAY WIV IT!'

Uh-oh. It was the Wind Rogue again. And she did not sound happy. Ray tried scrambling to her feet, but was knocked down by another HUGE gust. The Rogue then directed her hands towards the surrounding forest, sending a fierce blast of air ripping right through it, tearing tree trunks in half.

Ray covered her face with her hands as trees fell with almighty THUDS. The ground was squelched, plants were squished and animals ran away in terror. Then Ray noticed something else: wisps of black smoke rising up from the freshly torn trunks and heading her way. As these dark wisps approached, Ray was suddenly overwhelmed by a feeling of weakness.

'Shadow Essence!' she gasped.

'Let's see how you get on with THAT,' sneered the Wind Rogue, before surfing out of sight on a whirlwind of knickers.

'No, no!' cried Ray, clambering to her feet. But her knees buckled and she fell down again.

The back smoke slithered and snaked through the air towards Ray – a dark shadow hungry for her light. It was making her feel so tired. Using all of her energy, Ray heaved herself up, using her rainbow staff like a walking stick. But it was no good. She sat down next to one of the spiky tree stumps, and touched it lightly. She felt its emptiness, the sadness.

There was a shuffling nearby. Ray braced her staff, expecting to see the Wind Rogue again, but she was surprised to see a small girl. Her skin was a pale green and she had a mop of curly brown hair. Leaves were tucked behind a pointy ear. She looked at Ray with magenta-coloured eyes.

'You are a Rainbow Weatherling, aren't you?' the little girl asked politely.

'Oh, um, yes,' Ray replied. 'Who are you?'

'I am a Woodling,' said the girl.

A Woodling! Ray remembered reading about Woodlings in Rainbow Beard's letter.

To Ray's surprise, the Woodling squeaked with glee. 'You're the first Rainbow Weatherling in over a thousand years!' she said. 'We need you more than ever. Ever since Storm Tornadia, the bond between the Weatherlings and the Woodlings has been broken. Earth and sky are not meant to be so separate from one another. The Rainbow Weatherlings were the bridge between us. Now YOU are the bridge between us . . . Mother Nature's prophecy has finally come true! We have HOPE!'

'Mother Nature's prophecy?' asked Ray.

The tiny Woodling began to recite:

When stars disappear with shadow in hand
The powerless amid the Six will stand
Almost forgotten – a dynasty forsaken.
The bridge between Earth and sky
shall awaken.

'At every Eclipse, weather magic is at its strongest, especially inside the Weatherstone Circle,' continued the Woodling. 'The magic trapped inside the crystallised Shadow Essence will have sensed that YOU are a descendant of the Rainbow Weatherlings. It would have been fighting to return to a rightful host, unable to escape the grip of the Shadow Essence. But by standing inside the Circle on the most powerful night of the eleven-year cycle, it was enough to override the power of the Shadow Essence and set the rainbow weather magic free!'

'Wow,' said Ray. 'So that's how I got my magic!' Then she frowned. 'But what if this Shadow Essence absorbs my magic again?'

'You won't let it happen . . .' the Woodling said with a gentle smile. 'The Rainbow Weatherings of the past weren't ready for it, but YOU are.'

'I don't know,' sighed Ray. 'This Shadow Essence is strong, and I don't have the energy to escape it.'

The Woodling took Ray's hands in her own. They were small and soft, and Ray felt the warmth of the Woodling's touch flood through her.

'Oh my! You aren't just any Rainbow Weatherling,' said the Woodling, looking surprised. 'You have more magic inside you than

I expected!'

'Well, I kind of absorbed the magic of a whole clan,' muttered Ray, noticing tiny green sparkles dancing around their clasped hands. And suddenly she didn't feel so tired and weak any more.

Ray gasped as the green sparkles faded.

'Do you have magic too?'

The Woodling giggled. 'Weatherlings and Woodlings are more alike than you realise. While you make magic in the skies, we make forest magic down here.' She sighed. 'But without rainbow weather magic, we have not been able to save the trees, and without trees, us Woodlings grow weak. If the Rogues keep destroying forests we will eventually disappear, along with all the wildlife that live among us. But now you're here . . . we can save the forest. Together.'

'How?' asked Ray.

'Rain and sun must become one, then the forest sings and new life begins,' the Woodling spoke happily. 'Using your rainbow weather magic, you can combine sun and rain weather magic to breathe life into nature when it needs it most. But the spell is not complete without a Woodling's forest magic.'

'La Blaze can help us with the spell to save the trees,' cried Ray. 'She's a Sun Weatherling!'

But the Woodling looked unsure. 'Be careful, Rainbow,' she warned. 'Sometimes those you think are the strongest are in fact the weakest. THEY will need your help.'

Ray felt confused by these words. But before she could blink, the Woodling vanished into the forest foliage.

CHAPTER 23

GREAT HULKING BUMFACE!

Ray breathed in the woody scent of the trees and felt the softness of the green moss beneath her feet. Above her, Weather Warriors and Rogues zipped across the sky, and in the distance she could hear the tumbling of heavy trunks and the cracking of branches.

She had to find La Blaze! She couldn't be far away. Then they could save her family and friends and stop the Rogues together! Ray wished she knew where Nim was too.

She felt something wet splash her head.

'Pleeeease don't let that be bird poo,' she groaned, tentatively pressing her hand to her hair. 'Oh, phew, it's just water.'

Then she heard an almighty SPLOSH.

Ray knew that splosh.

'DROPLETT?!' she cried, when she saw the Rain Weatherling standing in a puddle, hands on her hips.

Ray ran as fast as she could to her friend and hugged her tightly.

'Oh, Droplett,' she cried. 'I didn't mean ANY of the horrid things I said earlier! I'm so sorry.'

Droplett smiled and wrapped her arms around her friend. 'I know you didn't.'

'I'm SO happy to see you!' Ray said, wiping a string of snot from her nose. 'But what are you doing here on Earth?'

'Well, THAT is a story,' said Droplett, shaking her head, 'A Wind Rogue kidnapped me.'

'What?!' cried Ray.

'I was sent spinning around in a swirling underwear nightmare. But luckily she underestimated my puddle-porting abilities,' Droplett explained. 'I was about to head back to the Weatherlands to find you, when I saw colours flashing across the sky and figured that HAD to be YOU. I don't know any other Weatherling who can do THAT!'

The friends hugged again.

'Droplett, I think Mum has been kidnapped too!' said Ray. 'Me and La Blaze flew here to find them, but then we got attacked in the sky by a pair of Thunder 'n' Lightning Rogues!'

Before Ray could say any more, the friends were almost blinded by the brightest light Ray had ever seen. She stumbled backwards, shielding her eyes with her arm, holding her rainbow staff in one hand and gripping Droplett's hand in the other. Little bright dots were dancing around behind her closed lids, and her cheeks were burning. As her eyes adjusted to the light, she saw the silhouette of a tall figure walking towards her.

'La Blaze!' Ray cried with relief as the Sun Weatherling glided into view. 'Thank the skies, you're OK! Look, I found Droplett! She got kidnapped by a Rogue too! That means my mum must be around here somewhere!'

La Blaze didn't answer.

There was a SPLASH, and a SPLODGE, then a ZAP and a rummmmmmmmmble, then a BAAAAAAH and a BOOOOOOM, as a whole bunch of Rogues landed one by one behind La Blaze. Not one weather instrument was in sight and they all had evil grins on their faces.

'Quick! La Blaze! BEHIND YOU!' Ray shouted, and tightened her grip on her rainbow staff.

La Blaze didn't look bothered at all. She was smiling. 'Oh,' she said, adjusting her jacket collar. 'Did I not introduce you to my friends?'

'F-friends?' Ray croaked.

The world entered slow-motion mode. Ray could hear Droplett shouting, but everything was muffled and fuzzy. Ray steadied herself, and her senses sharpened once again.

'. . . GREAT HULKING BUMFACE!' she heard Droplett finish shouting.

'Are you quite finished?' La Blaze replied, looking bored. She waved a hand and called out,

'Coo La Laaaaaaa!'

The posh pigeon emerged from within the surrounding trees rather ungracefully. He was carrying a large glass jar filled with something very, very dark indeed. He plonked it down at La Blaze's feet and bowed once, before swooping up to perch on her shoulder with his legs crossed.

La Blaze picked up the jar and twisted open the lid. She sank her hand deep into the black substance, grabbed a handful and let it trickle between her fingers.

Ray knew right away what it was. Shadow Essence. She could already feel it tugging at her magic. She dug her staff into the ground for balance.

'Who'd have thought . . .' said La Blaze, casually rubbing the black substance between her fingertips. 'Over a thousand years of Rogues trying to work out HOW Tornadia Twist did it, and the answer was all around us the whole time.'

Ray turned to Droplett. 'I never told La Blaze about the Shadow Essence, I promise!'

'I believe you, Ray,' said Droplett, not taking her eyes off La Blaze.

'You didn't *have* to tell me,' said La Blaze with an airy laugh. 'Why do you think I have a pigeon sidekick?'

Coo La La shook his head in disbelief, sending a black and white speckled feather floating to the forest floor. 'SIDEKICK?' he said. 'Is that all I am to you?'

Ray knew where she had seen a feather JUST like that before.

'YOU!' She pointed at the offended pigeon. '*You* were spying on us in the burrow! THAT'S why Snowden kept sneezing – he's allergic to you! And that's why Nim was acting so strange!' She frowned hard. 'AND you were in my *house* . . . What did you do with my mum?'

'Is this suddenly the *Point the Blame at Coo La La* SHOW?' the pigeon said, flying to the ground. 'If you MUST know, I simply shared a cup of tea with your mother. Then our good friend Squallia came to fetch her.'

A rush of wind swept through the clearing.

'Not again!' sighed Ray and Droplett in unison as the Wind Rogue with a love of knickers blasted through the trees.

Squallia was brandishing the biggest tornado Ray had ever seen. But this time, she hadn't just collected knickers. Trees and rocks swam around and around in the howling wind – and at the very bottom of the tornado were two figures. One of them had a mop of grey hair filled with tools. The other was a smaller figure with fuzzy white hair.

Ray's stomach dropped into her toes. It was her mum and Snowden, imprisoned within the wind, and powerless in the Rogue's formidable grip.

'LET THEM GO!' cried Ray, rushing towards Squallia with her rainbow staff. She pointed the staff at the Wind Rogue – but Squallia was quicker, waving a hand and sending both Ray and Droplett hurtling through the air.

'I wouldn't if I were you,' said La Blaze. Her expression was dark. 'You and your little drip-drop friend stand no chance against all of us.'

'AND YOU OWE ME NEW KNICKERS!' spat Squallia.

'In case you'd ALL forgotten,' shouted Droplett, clambering to her feet, 'RAY is a Rainbow Weatherling! She could take on ALL of you with *her* SUPER power!'

Ray gave Droplett an anxious actually-I-don't-think-I-could kind of glance.

'Ray might *possess* rainbow weather magic,' said La Blaze, folding her arms. 'But you all know that ANY weather magic requires practice. Ray here is yet to learn her craft. It would be VERY silly indeed to practise on my extremely talented team of Rogues.'

'I can't believe you tricked me!' said Ray in a wobbly voice, gazing up at the Weatherling who had been her hero. A mixture of anger and upset was bubbling up inside her belly. *Don't cry!* she told herself firmly. She swallowed hard. 'Droplett was right,' she said in as steady a voice as she could muster. 'I didn't really know you at all.'

La Blaze began to pace back and forth, arms behind her back. 'I'm willing to bargain with you,' she said nonchalantly.

Ray clenched her fists. 'If it's me you want, then fine. Just please let my mum and my friends go! They didn't ask for ANY of this.'

'No, Ray!' came Cloudia's muffled voice from the heart of Squallia's tornado.

'OH, Ray, Ray, Ray,' trilled La Blaze. 'I don't want *you*. I just want your MAGIC. You see . . . I was so close to BIG things. I was planning MY OWN storm! *STORM LA BLAZE!*' She threw her arms out theatrically. 'But then YOU went and unleashed the ancient rainbow weather magic – the ONE thing that threatens my plan.'

La Blaze spun around, staring at Ray with malice.

'But now I plan on finishing what Tornadia Twist started,' she hissed. 'When the Rainbow Weatherlings were drained of their magic all those years ago, nobody knew how Tornadia did it . . . And now I DO.'

Coo La La cleared his throat. 'THANKS to your *sidekick*'s impeccably good spying skills . . .'

La Blaze shooed the pigeon away. 'But this time,' she continued, 'I'll make sure there are no loose ends. Destroying the Earth's oldest and largest forest will create enough Shadow Essence to take away your rainbow weather magic – the last of its kind – FOREVER. And I shall make sure there's no risk of you *ever* finding it again.'

Ray dug her fingers into her palms.

'That's it, I'm gonna splosh her!' said Droplett, bracing her cape.

But she found herself circled by a flock of evil cloud-sheep with red eyes. Droplett prepared herself to puddle-port.

'One move and I'll send me flock to eat your little rainbow friend!' warned the Cloud Rogue.

Droplett frowned and folded her arms.

'You *can* make this easier for yourself,' La Blaze continued, focusing on Ray. 'Let me take your magic. I'll spare your friends and family . . . and you can go free. You've been magic-less before. You can do it again.'

The tornado of knickers and trees and foliage spun around Ray's mum and Snowden. The scary sheep-clouds surrounded Droplett. It was up to Ray to save them all!

'I'm not going to let you do this, La Blaze,' she said, feeling more angry than upset now. 'You're not taking my magic and I'm not letting you ruin this beautiful place. I thought you were an EARTH EXPLORER? You're meant to *love* this world. Not destroy it!'

La Blaze scoffed. 'Oh, Ray, you naïve little Weatherling . . . I had dreams once, just like you. Being born a Sun Weatherling meant I was destined for GREAT things! All I ever wanted was to BE someone. I *should* have been a powerful SunKeeper. Every day the humans would see MY light pouring down upon them. All of my family were SunKeepers – but I was the only one not to make the cut.' She frowned hard. 'So instead I decided to explore, find treasures, go on adventures, and see the world. I would write books and make my name known THAT way! But nobody cared about what I did. My books never sold. I was *nothing . . .*'

'FOGSWALLOP,' said Ray crossly. 'You were something to ME!'

A flicker of sadness flashed in La Blaze's eyes.

But the dark and determined expression soon returned.

'When I found the Rogues, I became *someone*!' La Blaze continued. 'Everybody respected me, noticed me. Rogues from all over knew my name. I worked my way up, helping other Rogues pursue their stormy dreams. And then it was finally my turn. My chance to lead my OWN storm, one that would have MY name attached to it. Soon, every Weatherling and every human will know the name *La Blaze* . . . I will go down in history, JUST like Eddie Blizzard or, better still, *Tornadia Twist*.' She leaned forward so that her face was inches away from Ray's. 'And I'm not going to let YOU get in the way.'

CHAPTER 24

WEATHER WARS

La Blaze's mob of Rogues surrounded Ray, hungry for action. Glowing orbs of electricity crackled above the Lightning Rogue's palms, while her thunder twin clenched his fists ready for rumbling. The Cloud Rogue kept her red-eyed cloud-sheep surrounding Droplett, and water poured from the hands of a stern-looking Rain Rogue. Behind them, a horde of angry snowmen marched their way through the trees, tearing them down with their hulking snow arms.

La Blaze was right. Ray couldn't possibly fight all of these Rogues by herself. The more they destroyed the forest around them, the more Shadow Essence snaked its way around her feet, weakening her, feeding on her magic.

But suddenly something caught Ray's

attention. Two beady eyes and a smiling mouth on one of the tree trunks directly behind the Rogues. Nim!

It took all of Ray's might not to shout out to him. With Nim, she'd be able to get off the ground, away from the threat of the Shadow Essence. She just needed to get to him.

'Let's get this over with, Ray,' La Blaze snarled. 'Just surrender that magic of yours. It's much easier to just give in and QUIT.'

Ray frowned. '*Quit*,' she muttered quietly. '*Quit?*' she said a little louder. 'If there's one thing I NEVER do . . . it's QUIT! And well – you said it yourself: *If at first the path you take is bumpy, there's always another path to finding the treasure!* There's ALWAYS another path!'

Ray focused all of her energy on her rainbow staff.

'What are you doing?' asked La Blaze. 'You can't possibly beat us . . . beat ME!'

Ray swung the staff over her head, then back again, with one big WHOOOOOOOOSH.

A huge arc of colours stretched through the air over the Rogues' heads. Ray bent her knees and jumped, sliding across the length of the rainbow – over the VERY baffled-looking Rogues – straight on to a fully formed Nim's floofy back with a satisfying SQUIDGE!

Next Ray pointed her staff towards the flock of evil cloud-sheep surrounding Droplett. With another huge stream of colours, Ray took control, concentrating hard. One by one, the sheep's eyes stopped glowing, and the flock began to skip merrily around Droplett, who cheered with joy.

The Rogues all stared at the dancing cloud-sheep. Up and down they jumped, around and around . . . and around . . . Slowly but surely, the Rogues' eyelids began to droop. Everyone knew that counting sheep sent you to sleep!

'Quick, Droplett!' urged Ray. 'I can't hold the sheep for long . . .'

The little Rain Weatherling grabbed her cape and puddle-ported, appearing beside Ray on Nim's back just as Ray's grip on the cloud weather magic wore off. The rainbow colours disappeared, and the cloud-sheep exploded, snapping the Rogues out of their hypnotic daydream.

La Blaze shook her head and glared at Ray. Her hands began to glow. Ray noticed La Blaze was no longer wearing the sunflowers on her wrists. This made her magic WAY more unpredictable. 'I refuse to be beaten by a ten-year-old girl with rainbow hair!' she spat. 'You've given me no choice . . .'

La Blaze glowed brighter. It hurt Ray's eyes, but she refused to back down.

'I can't see!' cried Droplett, shielding her face. Nim miaowed and made his own eyes disappear into his floofy head for protection.

'La Blaze, stop!' Ray urged.

La Blaze wasn't listening. She lifted both arms up into the air, glowing brighter still.

'Come on, Nim,' said Ray. 'I need you to do your best flying now!'

Nim purred and revved himself up, ascending through the treetops and into the skies. Down below, the tornado still whirled furiously around Cloudia and Snowden.

'I need to find a way to save Mum and Snowden!' cried Ray.

'I could try puddle-porting into the tornado to get them out?' suggested Droplett.

Ray shook her head. 'Too dangerous . . . There HAS to be a way!'

Far below, something crackled and roared.

Wind howled. A thick grey mist engulfed the sky as more evil cloud-creatures approached from every direction.

'This is NOT good,' muttered Droplett, gripping on to Nim's back.

The cloud-cat hissed at the other not-so-cute clouds and flicked his tail warily.

Ray felt the wind pick up and icy hail began to fall. 'Nim, we need to fly like we've never flown before!' she cried.

The cloud-cat swerved from side to side, avoiding the lumps of ice cutting through the air. Fizzes of electricity sizzled and zipped past Ray's

ears. Rain began to pour sideways, making it
really hard to fly.

'EURGH! This is the WORST kind of rain!'
cried Droplett, trying to counteract the sidepour
with her own rain weather magic.

It was getting harder to fly and harder to see.
Ray wondered if she'd bitten off more than she
could chew. She couldn't give up. Maybe she
could calm the weather using her rainbow weather
magic . . . But a HUGE thrash of wind almost
ripped her staff from her grip.

'WATCH OUT!' yelped Droplett as a purple
lightning bolt headed straight for Ray's bottom.

Ray swerved Nim out of the way just in time.

The sky grew darker and the air became sticky and humid. An explosion of bright light erupted from the forest. Ray gasped in horror as tree upon tree fell victim to La Blaze's team of Rogues, leaving behind thick black wisps that trickled their way upwards like growing tentacles.

Nim flew the friends higher. Ray couldn't see the forest any more as the murky mist thickened and the dirty storm clouds raged.

'Ray!' squeaked Droplett, pointing below.

Rising up from the stormy mass emerged La Blaze, riding on the back of another sun-dragon she had created using her sun magic. Ray gulped. This time it was bigger and brighter than before. As La Blaze approached, Ray noticed the jar of Shadow Essence cradled in one arm and Coo La La on her shoulder.

La Blaze's eyes were wild with fury. 'You will not DESTROY MY DREAM!' she screamed.

The sun-dragon opened its mouth to release a flare of fiery light. Ray ducked and Nim swerved so sharply that he ended up exploding.

The friends went tumbling through the rain and ice and mist. Ray's long hair tangled around her arms, as she desperately gripped her rainbow staff. She was falling and spinning, unable to work out which way was up. Any moment now she'd hit the ground, and cause quite possibly the BIGGEST bottom bruise she'd ever had.

WHOOOOOOOOOOOSH!

Suddenly Ray wasn't falling any more. She was moving upwards at an alarming rate. There was something HUGE and white and fluffy beneath her. But it wasn't Nim.

'OMELETTE!' she heard a familiar voice shout, followed by a SPLAT!

'DAD!' cried Ray.

She and Droplett were sprawled across the back of Waldo the cloud-whale, who was swimming through the gloomy sky. Haze was guiding the cloud-whale with his long crook in one hand and throwing eggs with the other hand. One egg hit La Blaze right between the eyes.

'This ain't NO YOLK!' shouted Ray's dad with a cheeky side wink at Ray. 'These omelettes have come in very useful!'

Ray didn't have the heart or the time to tell her dad that they were called eggs.

'Nice hair!' shouted Haze, glancing back at his daughter. 'We've got a LOT to catch up on!' He swerved Waldo away from an onslaught of cloud-monkeys.

'If we get home in one piece!' shrieked Ray as an orb of glowing light narrowly missed her head.

La Blaze screamed with rage, trying to wipe the egg from her face. Seizing the opportunity, Ray pointed her rainbow staff at the disgruntled Sun Rogue. As the colours of the rainbow worked their way across the sky towards the sun-dragon, Ray felt its power surge through her. It was INTENSE. She had to use every ounce of energy to harness the strength of La Blaze's power in her rainbow grip.

Ray pulled her staff towards her as if hauling a huge lever. Slowly but surely, the sun-dragon began to wibble and change shape. La Blaze waved her arms around in a fluster, so that it looked as if she were attempting some kind of interpretive dance. She stared at Ray in shock.

'MY MAGIC!' she shrieked. 'STOP THAT!'

But Ray kept going, concentrating with all her might on the sun magic in her grasp until finally the sun-dragon had transformed into something MUCH less intimidating.

'Is that a . . . sun-slug?' asked Haze.

La Blaze was looking rather silly on the back of

the big fat sun-slug, lolloping around in the air. '*What the fog?*' she cried.

Coo La La held his face in his wings. 'This is BEYOND embarrassing. I cannot be seen here,' he cooed before flying away.

'DON'T LEAVE ME, YOU POSH LITTLE SKY-RAT!' La Blaze howled.

Ray watched in horror as La Blaze tossed the open jar of Shadow Essence through the air with all her might. The black substance slithered towards Ray, absorbing all the rainbow colours. All at once, Ray felt La Blaze's sun magic slip from her grasp.

'REVERSE, REVERSE!' Haze urged Waldo, waving his cloud-crook frantically.

But as fast as the cloud-whale swam through the sky, the Shadow Essence was faster. The dense black nightmare hit Ray like a ton of ice.

She hadn't realised how much her rainbow weather magic was a part of her until it was slowly being taken away.

'RAAAAAAY!' she heard Droplett shouting, but everything was distant, and Ray felt herself fall backwards, and down, down, down.

CHAPTER 25

I WON'T GIVE UP!

Ray opened her eyes. She was lying on the muddy ground. On Earth. She felt so . . . empty.

'This is very pretty,' said La Blaze's voice in an airy tone. 'Shame you won't be needing it any more.'

Ray pulled herself into a seated position – and gasped. La Blaze was holding her rainbow staff. Droplett and Haze were now stuck inside Squallia's huge tornado alongside Cloudia and Snowden.

'And NO puddle-porting,' Squallia hissed at Droplett.

Droplett looked to Ray sadly and mouthed the words, 'I'm sorry.'

But Ray was the one who was sorry. Everyone she loved was trapped. And it was all her fault.

'How much more Shadow Essence are we gonna need to drain all of her magic, boss?' asked Squallia, rubbing her hands together hungrily.

La Blaze studied her nails. 'Target the older trees first. Their Shadow Essence will be stronger,' she said darkly. 'If that's not enough, take down the whole forest.'

'No!' croaked Ray. But it was barely a whisper.

Using her powerful sun magic, La Blaze conjured up a *three*-headed, glowing sun-dragon. She laughed evilly as she swung her arms around and sent the HUGE creature snaking its way through the surrounding forest, its fiery breath scorching through trees like a hungry serpent. Torrents of Shadow Essence spilled from the heart of the ruined tree stumps, twisting towards Ray like slippery, slithering nightmares.

Darkness, emptiness. Ray felt herself grow weaker.

'RAAAAAAAAAAAY! You can fight this!' she heard a voice call out, but it was so far away.

The colours in Ray's hair began to slowly fade.

'RAY! You're strong!' said another voice.

'I don't know if I am,' Ray whispered.

Then she heard, 'Ray Grey DOESN'T give up! And that's what makes you powerful!'

A spark of something fizzled inside Ray.

I don't give up, she thought. Weather magic or no weather magic.

'I WON'T give up . . .' she said out loud.

Using all of her strength, Ray got to her feet.

There was still magic inside her. She could feel it. She just had to focus on it. Without her staff, it was much harder to control. But she had nothing to lose now.

Ray let her rainbow weather magic flood through her body and out through her fingertips, hurtling towards the tornado around her family and friends. The colours weren't as bright and her magic wasn't full strength, but Ray felt the rush of wind hit her as she harnessed the Wind Rogue's power.

'NOT AGAIN!' shrieked Squallia.

Ray squeezed her hands into fists as quickly and as tightly as she could. The tornado disappeared in a POOF of knickers and branches, setting her friends and family free.

But the effort had been immense. Ray felt her knees wobble.

Droplett emerged with a splosh from a puddle next to her.

'We're coming, Ray!' shouted Cloudia, as she and Ray's dad swept across the clearing on the back of Waldo the cloud-whale while Snowden was busy conjuring snowballs and knocking every Rogue to their hands and knees.

'ROGUES! GET UP AND STOP THEM AT ONCE!' shrieked La Blaze.

The Rogues tried to get to their feet.

'We can't, boss!' cried the Rain Rogue. 'We're STUCK!'

Snowden waltzed to Ray's other side, waving around the Stenchamite Stalk he'd been keeping in his bag. 'Told you, you just never know when the sticky sap might come in handy!'

'This is preposterous!' La Blaze screamed.

Ray was sure the Sun Rogue would explode
with anger at any second, and Ray felt so tired.
She closed her eyes for a second.

Something warm gently took her hand. Then it
took her other hand. She felt something flutter in
her tummy. An energy.

Ray flicked open her eyes. Droplett and
Snowden were standing by her side, each holding
her hand. Beside them, holding their hands, stood
her parents. And – POOF – there was Nim too,
appearing on Ray's head with a joyful MIAOW.

Ray squeezed her friends' hands. She FELT Snowden's sparkly snow magic and Droplett's energetic rain magic surging through her, and through her friends, she could also feel her dad's cloud magic. She felt her mum's determination – and something that the Shadow Essence couldn't take away. LOVE.

The love from her friends, and the love from her mum and dad.

Ray's heart felt as if it might burst. She saw the colours rush through her mind. She saw familiar faces . . . friendly faces with rainbow-coloured hair, and one very long rainbow-coloured beard. Her family from the past.

Ray knew who she really was.

She was Rainbow Grey.

And with one last PUSH, she let the biggest brightest rainbow BURST out from her hands and wrap itself around La Blaze.

'But . . . the Shadow Essence!' La Blaze yelled. 'Why isn't it working?!'

Ray smiled. 'Because rainbow weather magic is more than just controlling the magic of others,' she said. 'It's more than making rainbow slides. Sure, on its own Shadow Essence might consume me, but TOGETHER with my friends and family, it can't touch me. And the one thing a rainbow can do more than any other magic, is give everyone HOPE. And hope is what keeps everyone going.

Shadow Essence can't take that away!'

'You won't beat me!' cried La Blaze, but she dropped the rainbow staff and her voice broke. 'Being a Rogue is all I have . . .'

CHAPTER 26

MY HERO

Suddenly, La Blaze didn't seem so scary any more. Ray heard the Woodling's words in her mind.

'*Sometimes those you think are the strongest are in fact the weakest. THEY will need your help.*'

Ray knew what she had to do. She let go of her friends' hands and stepped forward.

'Ray! What are you doing?' cried Cloudia.

'It's OK, Mum,' said Ray.

She picked up her rainbow staff in one hand, and offered the other hand to La Blaze. 'That's not true,' she said.

'What's not true?' La Blaze croaked.

'That being a Rogue is all you have,' said Ray. 'You have so much more. I've looked up to you my whole life.

You changed my world. It was because of YOU that I went to find that treasure, because I wanted to be *just* like you. A brave, daring, adventurous Earth Explorer!'

La Blaze lowered her gaze. Her sun magic dimmed a little.

'And if it wasn't for you,' Ray went on, 'then I may never have found my rainbow weather magic at all. You've inspired me so much.'

The light dimmed a little more.

'I just wanted to be noticed,' La Blaze said quietly.

'*I* noticed you,' said Ray.

La Blaze frowned. 'You're just *one* Weatherling.'

'So?' said Ray. 'I was one Weatherling without any magic, but YOU gave me courage. You made me feel like I could still do BIG things, no matter what.'

'Ha! Well, everything turned out all right for you, didn't it?' La Blaze scoffed. 'Now you're going to be the most famous Weatherling in the Weatherlands!'

I don't want to be the most famous Weatherling,' said Ray. 'And I still have so much to learn. Sure, I have all of this new magic, but I don't know how to use it properly, or just how much power is inside me. But I won't give up, because I think of all the BIG adventures you've been on and how you never gave up.'

'It may take a little longer, but you'll get there in the end,' La Blaze finished, her voice much softer now.

'Everything takes me a while,' said Ray with a shrug. 'But it's always worth it.'

The edges of La Blaze's lips crept into a small smile. 'I was never great at sun weather magic, Ray,' she said, as the last of her light went out to reveal Haze, Cloudia, Droplett and Snowden all standing by Ray's side.

'I don't know . . . that was a pretty epic sun-dragon you made!' muttered Droplett.

La Blaze sighed. 'It's nothing compared to making the big Sunflower in the sky glow. When I failed to become a SunKeeper, I felt unworthy.

I was so desperate to prove myself.'

'My mum told me I don't have to prove myself to ANYONE,' said Ray, looking to Cloudia with a smile. 'And anyway, you're not unworthy just because not everyone knows your name. You'll always be *my* hero.'

La Blaze's eyes grew glossy.

'So what do you say?' asked Ray hopefully. 'Start over? Because I'd *really* love you to write that book about me!'

La Blaze chuckled lightly and took Ray's hand.

'Let's start over,' she said.

'WAIT,' came the muffled voice of Bop, the Thunder Rogue still stuck firmly in the Stenchamite sap. 'DOES THIS MEAN WE'RE NOT MAKING A STORM NO MORE?'

La Blaze gave a shy smile. 'The storm is off, guys.'

'Oh, thank the skies,' said Bop's Lightning twin, Blap. 'It's the final round of *The Wind Wars* quiz on the Fizzogram tonight. I've been looking forward to it all week.'

'Oh, is that TONIGHT?!' gasped Squallia.

The Rogues started to chat among themselves.

'I hate to bring this conversation down a level,' said Haze. 'And I am very glad we've worked things out and that you'll get to catch up on *The Wind Wars* quiz. . . But this doesn't change the fact that you've destroyed a LOT of this forest.'

La Blaze bit her lip and Ray looked at the broken landscape sadly. Then she remembered the Woodling's words. *We can save the forest. Together!*

'Together . . .' Ray whispered with a smile. She gripped her rainbow staff. 'There's still hope!' she said, before looking up at La Blaze. 'But I'm going to need your help.'

'Me?' La Blaze said in surprise.

'Yes,' said Ray. 'Rain and sun must become one, then the forest sings and new life begins . . .'

Droplett's ears pricked. 'RAIN!' she said. 'I can help with that part!'

'But what about all the Shadow Essence still coming out of the broken trees?' asked Snowden with concern. 'If your magic goes near it, Ray . . .'

Ray spotted a green sparkle among the tired landscape. 'I think I'll be OK,' she said with a smile. 'The Rainbow Weatherlings of the past didn't know what they were dealing with, but I DO. And well, I believe I have some extra help . . .' She nodded towards the green twinkles.

Then Ray held her staff up high and said with confidence, 'Together we are stronger!'

'Let's breathe some life back into this place,' said Droplett, bracing her rain cape.

La Blaze nodded and put on her sunflower wristbands to channel her magic properly.

'Let's do this,' she said as the sunflowers began to glow.

Ray let her rainbow weather magic pour from her staff, then felt La Blaze's sunshine magic and Droplett's rain magic pulse through her.

Once she had a firm grip on their power, Ray pointed her rainbow staff towards the felled forest.

Focusing on the energy flowing through her,

Ray let a beautiful rainbow pour from her staff across the sky. A shower of bright red, orange, yellow, green, indigo and violet rained down on the ruined trees.

'Is it working?!' asked Droplett. Colours rained down, but the trees were still very much broken.

'Nothing is happening,' said Ray, losing hope. 'Maybe I was too ambitious?' But she shook the feelings of doubt away and pushed on forward. 'I WON'T give up!'

'Look!' cried La Blaze. 'Something IS happening!'

Amid the black and grey of the torn and twisted tree stumps, tiny green sparkles flickered and glimmered against the darkness.

'Yes! The Woodlings!' whispered Ray.

'Woodlings?' said La Blaze.

Ray watched as the Woodlings' forest magic danced across the desolate landscape, the green glimmers weaving around Ray's rainbow colours. Like tiny beacons of hope shimmering against the darkness, Ray spotted a young sapling begin to emerge from the ground. Then another one sprouted up, and another, and another, until the forest was filled with the beginnings of life.

As the magic unfurled around her, Ray smiled. Then she turned to her parents.

'So, Muuuum,' she said sheepishly. 'Are you still angry at me for sneaking to Earth twice?'

'You did it TWICE?' gasped her dad.

Cloudia pulled Ray into a hug. 'I think saving us all might make up for it.'

Ray and her parents hugged tightly, soon joined by Droplett and Snowden.

La Blaze stood awkwardly by herself. Coo La La landed in front of her on the muddy ground and spread out his wings.

'Go on then,' he said, rolling his eyes.

La Blaze and the pigeon hugged. Then Ray pulled them into the group.

'What did Rainbow Beard say at the end of his letter?' said Droplett. '*For every rainbow, a Storm WILL follow* .'

The Weatherlings looked at her with wide eyes.

'No, wait,' said Droplett. 'It's the other way round. *For every storm, a rainbow WILL follow!'*

Ray grinned and held her rainbow staff up high. 'Well, there is one rainbow spell I think I've almost got the hang of!' she said.

She swung the staff forwards and backwards, making the biggest, BRIGHTEST arc of colours. And for the first time in a thousand years, Earth saw a rainbow stretching across the sky.

'Now you're just showing off,' said Snowden.

'That's not showing off,' said Ray. 'THIS is!'

She jumped up into the air and surfed across the colours, arms held high, with Nim zipping along behind her. Then she shouted as loud as she could.

'I AM *RAINBOW GREEEEEEY AND I WILL – oops!'*

Ray tripped over, rolled off the end of the rainbow and landed on Nim, who promptly exploded.

CHAPTER 27
SPLAT

'So what do we do now?' asked Droplett.

The friends were curled up in the centre of the secret burrow beneath the Rainbow Weatherstone. The sparkling sunflower lanterns cast a warm glow upon the place, and the wind chimes jingled lightly. A picnic was set out on a shallow stump in the centre of the burrow, adorned with lightning scones, pitter-patter pancakes, sizzling snowdrop slices and breezy bogbites. (Nobody really liked those, but somehow they ended up a part of every picnic.)

It had been a few days since La Blaze had unleashed her raging storm on the world, and Earth had seen its nicest weather yet. Mostly because a lot of the Rogues were busy listening to episodes of *The Wind War*s quiz on catch-up.

'I guess we carry on as normal?' Ray answered

with a shrug. 'School and stuff . . .'

Ray's parents had let Ray have a few days off school to recover from her action-packed weekend. The head teacher Mrs Glacielle had been made fully aware of Ray's new weather magic, and had agreed that Ray's afternoons could be spent practising in the secret burrow with La Blaze's help.

'Y'know,' said Droplett through a mouthful of lightning scone, 'in all the weather comics I've read, I always wondered what the heroes did after their epic world-saving moment. Everything afterwards seems a bit MEH.'

'Who's to say we won't have another epic adventure?' said Ray with a wink.

'I don't know if I can take something THAT epic for a while,' said Snowden, grabbing two drizzle-pickle sandwiches. 'And I'm not doing anything until I actually finish a WHOLE sandwich without it getting wet!'

A KNOCK KNOCK KNOCK echoed through the burrow.

'They're here!' sang Ray.

She grabbed her rainbow staff and shouted the word 'BEARD!' Within seconds, her mum and dad came whizzing down the rainbow slide, arms up in the air, screaming with joy, followed by Waldo who floofed his way down grumpily.

'It looks GORGEOUS in here!' gushed Cloudia, gazing around the burrow. Ray could tell her mum was trying to work out what she could build and decorate.

'Ray-Ray, this is wonderful!' said Haze, settling himself down and adding a few eggs to the picnic.

'We're going to make this our special secret hang-out!' said Droplett.

'Well, that sounds brilliant! And before I forget,' said Cloudia, rummaging around in her mop of hair and pulling out a long silver thread, 'no secret base is complete without a silver lining, eh?'

She wove the lining around the roots of the burrow so that they shimmered and sparkled in the sunflower lanterns' light.

Ray watched as her best friends and her family munched their way through the picnic, chatting and laughing together. Nim decided to prance around the ceiling with the tiny cloud-sheep . . . or he could have been chasing them. Ray wasn't sure. All she knew was that she didn't want this moment to end.

Cloudia shuffled up next to Ray and put an arm around her daughter. 'So our great ancestor Mr Beardy, or whatever he's called, was the head of a whole Rainbow SCHOOL?' she said with a whistle. 'I wonder where the school used to be?'

'Who knows!' said Ray, leaning her head on her mum's chest. 'I wish I could go to Rainbow School to learn how to use my magic properly.'

'Well, it looks like you have everything you need to know right here.' Cloudia gestured to the walls covered in Rainbow Beard's teachings. 'And maybe YOU will follow in Beardy's footsteps and be the head of your OWN Rainbow school one day!' She winked.

Ray blew a raspberry, 'I have a ton to learn before I stand a chance of teaching anyone anything,' she said. 'I mean, look at ALL those notes and weather spells. I don't know how above Earth I'm going to remember them ALL. Not to mention the fact I have a bazillion rainbow gifts and no clue how to use them!'

Haze tapped Ray on the nose affectionately.

'You might have lots to learn, Ray-Ray,' he said, 'but you don't have to do this alone, remember.'

'YEAH! We're gonna help you as much as we can!' said Droplett, giving Ray a friendly nudge.

'Anyway, we made a promise,' Snowden added. 'To support each other no matter what!' Droplett nodded in agreement.

Ray's heart swelled. 'Thank you,' she said. 'You guys are the BEST.'

'Oh, we know!' said Droplett with a wink, swishing her cape and soaking poor Snowden's last bite of drizzle-pickle sandwich. 'Oh . . . oops . . . sorry, Snowden.' She winced.

But Snowden smiled. 'It's OK . . . I've realised it's not a TRUE drizzle-pickle sandwich if it's not a bit soggy.'

The friends burst into a fit of giggles, before there was another knock from above.

'S'MEEEEE!' shouted a familiar voice. 'Your ex-arch-nemesis!'

'Do you think she'll always call herself that?' asked Droplett, raising an eyebrow.

There was a 'WEEEEEEEEEEEEEEEEEE!' as La Blaze came sliding down the rainbow slide into the burrow.

'Sorry I'm late,' said the Sun Weatherling, dusting herself down. She gazed at her surroundings. 'Wow, this place is CUTE!'

After the 'forest incident' La Blaze had made an official apology to the Council of Forecasters and the Weatherlands, declaring that her stormy days were behind her. She'd made a promise that she would help Ray on her journey to becoming a great Rainbow Weatherling.

'Where's Coo La La?' asked Ray, looking for the posh pigeon.

'Oh, he was offended about the whole SIDEKICK remark,' said La Blaze. 'So he's taking a mini seaside break on Earth to recover.'

Snowden let out a small sigh of relief, clearly glad not to have to deal with his pigeon allergy.

'Oooh, I have something to show you!' La Blaze rummaged around in a large bag she had hanging over her shoulder and pulled out a book.

'I've started writing my new book.'

Ray stared at the cover with the shiny title and felt her heart skip a beat. It said: '*Rainbow Grey. The Weatherling Who Never Gave Up.*'

'I want to tell YOUR story Ray,' said La Blaze. 'You always say how I inspired you, but the truth is, it's the other way around. And well, I think that your story will inspire others too.'

Ray didn't know what to say. So she did what she knew how to do best and gave La Blaze a great big hug. But then a very deep grumble interrupted the moment.

'Please tell me that was a hunger sound?' asked Droplett, looking alarmed.

Another grumble, louder this time.

'Um, La Blaze, it seems to be coming from your bag,' said Ray.

'Oh, that's odd!' The Sun Weatherling pulled a large box out from inside the bag, with the word RISING BUN BAKERY printed across the lid. 'I completely forgot I'd fetched these on the way . . .' she added with a smile. 'Seems they come with added sound effects!'

'Um, La Blaze, I don't suppose you bought something called a rumblebun, did you?' asked Ray cautiously as she and her friends slowly backed away.

'How did you know?!' asked La Blaze. 'I actually bought TEN!'

'Oh my . . .' muttered Snowden, holding up his *Anthology of Snowflakes* to shield his face.

'Droplett, we might need a puddle portal . . . NOW!' cried Ray as the rumblebuns began to wibble and wobble violently inside the box.

'What's wrong?' asked La Blaze. 'Who wants to try one?' She grabbed the edge of the lid.

'No! Don't open the –'

SPLAT!

'. . . box,' Ray finished, completely covered from head to toe in rumblebun goo.

Nim miaowed happily and began licking the bright pink syrup off everyone's faces.

'Well,' said Ray, giggling as the cloud-cat licked her ears. 'Nothing like an explosive end to the day!' And with that, Nim also exploded.

THE END

EPILOGUE

Coo La La watched the tide move in and out slowly, listening to the sound of the gentle waves as the big Sunflower in the sky disappeared beyond the horizon. He was sitting on a sandcastle, having commandeered it from a rather rude seagull.

'One day I won't be the sidekick,' he said with a yawn. 'I'll the be STAR of the show.'

A shooting star zipped across the night sky towards him. It got brighter and brighter and it was heading STRAIGHT for the beach.

Coo La La scrambled to his feet as it hit the beach with force, sending a huge cloud of sand into the air. The pigeon hid behind his sandcastle, peeking out from behind one of the crumbling turrets.

As the sand settled, Coo La La saw a tall woman with black and white stripy hair twisted into a pile on her head and vivid eyes; one purple and one blue.

'Well, well, well,' she said in a playful tone.

'This place looks just as pathetic as it did a thousand years ago.'

She lifted her arms, creating a whirlwind of sand mixed with thunder and lightning, then brought her fist down on to the gritty ground. A huge crack zigzagged across the beach. Coo La La's castle slipped into the crack, exposing the bewildered pigeon.

'OH, hello,' said the woman, her eyes wild and curious.

Coo La La kept a safe distance. 'I'm not interested in being your sidekick if that's what you're about to ask,' he said flatly, flapping over to perch on a large shell. 'Who are you?'

'Me?' said the woman, skimming a pebble across the water nonchalantly. She smiled a cool but wicked smile. 'My name is Tornadia. Tornadia Twist. And I have BIG plans . . .'

Look out for the next whirlwind adventure with Ray and her friends, coming soon!